A G

MW01196731

By: EL Griffin

Saint

This shit was killing me. I wasn't used to sitting back and not being able to take action. All I wanted to do was make the pain go away and tell Nya things would get better. But there wasn't a damn thing I could say or do that would make a difference right now.

The only thing I could do was hold shit down and be here for her. She could always count on me for that.

Nya was like a little sister to me. Her and my younger sister Jolie had been rocking since they were in the first grade.

We all grew up together and were close as hell even as we got older. Since day one, I acted as her protector and tried to take care of her like an older brother. But over the years my feelings changed.

Now when I looked at her, the last thing I saw was the little ass girl she used to be. She was beautiful in every way to me. From her face to her banging ass body, that already filled out like a grown ass woman at the age of

15. There wasn't a bitch around that compared or even came close in my eyes.

More than her looks, she was real.

But, I never let shit go further than friendship between us and I never planned to. I wasn't trying to be serious with any bitch ever. That love and relationship shit was the downfall of too many niggas. Fuck that. She deserved better.

I shouldn't be thinking about that shit right now with everything going on anyway. But I was still a nigga after all and being around her sexy ass didn't help.

What I couldn't handle, was sitting in here watching her hold back tears like she had been doing for the past few hours. That was really fucking with me. I couldn't stand to see her like this.

I sat back smoking some OG Kush, kicked back in a chair at the small ass table my granddaddy kept in his old shotgun house. I needed to smoke some shit to keep from losing my mind or wilding the fuck out.

Otherwise I might end up murdering any nigga that stepped to me wrong when I headed back out on the block later.

I looked over at Nya again and this time her eyes were trained right on me. She had been crying on and off most of the day, but since we had been back she held that shit in.

She looked at me with that expression she always had when we were alone. No matter if her parent's death was heavy on her mind or not, I still saw the love she had for me.

Usually I wouldn't look at her for too long or let her see that I felt the same way. But tonight was different, shawty was hurting. Maybe I could make her feel better.

For once, I didn't look away. It was the least I could give her right now.

She got up and walked over to where I was, invading my personal space, stepping right in front of me. I could smell that sweet ass perfume her ass always wore, that smelled like peaches and cream.

She reached out, taking the blunt out of my hand. I let her get it and she went ahead and took a few pulls before handing it back.

Nya took another step closer, putting herself right between my damn legs, her body coming in contact with mine.

My dick was hard as fuck and I knew her pussy was just as wet. The mothafucka was sitting in my face. But I played shit off and kept looking straight ahead at my phone in my other hand.

Nya's ass wasn't having that shit though, she wanted my full attention. She grabbed the phone out of my hand and set it on the table.

Normally I wouldn't let a bitch come up on me the way Nya was, not even her ass. But I wasn't trying to have her ass in here crying and shit again.

Out of habit I brushed my hand over my fresh waves and then looked up from the small ass chair I was sitting in.

I tried thinking about any fucking thing else, besides this damn beautiful ass girl standing with her thick ass legs and pussy in my face.

I took another pull of the blunt then put it out. I was looking for an out, any fucking thing. I even tried listening for some noise that meant Jolie finally brought her ass back home.

That way I could make an exit and get the fuck up out of this house before I did some shit I would regret.

Nya being all close with her body on mine was pushing the limits. She knew what the fuck she was doing. There was only so much temptation a nigga could take.

But I couldn't give in. No matter what, I needed to get the fuck up outa here.

My mind and my dick weren't cooperating at all. There wasn't a sound, no distractions to interfere with Nya or her body tempting the fuck outa me.

I looked up again, enough to look her in the face. Nya had my ass stuck.

She slid both her hands down the sides of my face and kept her soft ass fingers resting on my jaw.

I guess she had some shit to get off her chest. I didn't have shit to say to shawty. I wasn't a quiet nigga, but right now my damn voice was caught.

"You know what it is Saint. Stop actin' like you ain't got no feeling's fo' me. I see the way you look at me when you think no one's watching." Nya said, looking serious as hell.

Damn what the fuck could I say to that shit? Yeah I was feeling her. Shit the way Nya had me was some other shit that I wasn't even trying to think about and definitely not let her know about.

I didn't even admit how deep my feelings were for her, to my damn self. I wasn't trying to take shit there with her. So I did the one thing I knew to do and that was lie my ass off.

I wasn't built for that love shit. I never planned on settling down or letting a bitch have a hold on me. I wasn't the nigga for her. I needed to make her realize the shit she was speaking on wasn't gonna happen.

"I'm not 'bout to play with you, ya heard meh. You're like a lil' sista to me shawty. It's some fucked up shit you goin' through... but I ain't that nigga." *I said serious as hell while I stood to get up.*

"Really! You gon' say that shit to my face. Tell me you don't care about me then. That you don't want me, like I want you. Tell me straight up to my face. I wanna hear that

8

shit." She all but yelled at me, causing her voice to crack, while she held back more tears.

I wasn't about to sit here and be tempted no more or watch her cry again. As soon as I stood up, Nya backed up a few more steps and crossed her arms over her chest. I saw a few tears escape her eyes and fall over her cheeks.

My train of thought was sidetracked when I noticed her hard nipples and big titties sitting up nice through the white shirt she had on.

Even after I lied my ass off, I still wanted to grab ahold of her and touch every inch of her body. Especially now that she put shit out there and told me how she felt for real.

She brought that shit to the light and now that it was out, I could have easily said fuck it and gave her the dick.

Instead, I grabbed my wallet off the table and threw my fitted on, before walking towards the door. I needed to get the fuck away from Nya's ass.

"I'm 'bout to get up outa here, my dip 'bout to come through. You can still wait for Jolie." I told her over my shoulder as I walked towards the front door, like she didn't just say the shit she did.

I knew I was being an ass, and it was fucked up the way I came at her, but I did and said whatever the fuck I needed to in order to *look out for her. Even if the shit hurt her now, she would be better off for it later.*

Before I made it to the front door of the small ass house, Nya stormed past me and out of the fucking door.

Shawty didn't even give a second look back in my direction. Shit, I couldn't blame her. She put herself out there, and I shut that shit down.

She was going through some of the worst shit a person could go through, but I wasn't the nigga for her, so it was better if she hated my ass than thought we were gonna be together.

-Winter 2018-

NyAsia (Nya)

I sat on the stool looking at the reflection in the mirror looking back at me. I should have recognized myself. But I honestly didn't know who the fuck I was anymore.

I finished applying my lipstick before popping my heart-shaped lips and standing up to get a better look at myself in my outfit for tonight.

I didn't have time to feel sorry for myself or be in my damn feelings about the shit. This was my life, like it or not, and I had responsibilities to take care of.

I would never let my little brother go without. Since our parents' death both our lives had been turned upside down.

But I made sure that through all the fucked up shit, he didn't suffer or go without. So when my fraudulent ass auntie first started with the abuse and neglect I made a decision that it was time for my own childhood to end.

I needed to step up and take care of Terrell since he was so young and couldn't do shit for himself. My brother was everything to me.

I woke up every day with one thing that kept me focused and that was taking care of Terrell. Everything I did since that day was for him. Every boost I made, every lick, every fucking thing.

I did just about anything to keep us both fed and keep him laced in the best shit. I would gladly go without if it meant he was straight.

That was why I looked a mess half the time. I wasn't worried about that shit though. My hustle had gotten us this far and I wasn't about to stop making shit happen.

There were only two things I hadn't done to make some bread and that was sell pussy or strip. Yeah I tricked off niggas from time to time, but I never gave up the pussy unless we were in a relationship.

Even if all my relationships were missing the emotions and love on my end. I never gave my heart away to these niggas. I didn't even think I had a heart left to give if I wanted to.

I never stripped because I wasn't confident with my looks like that, to be out there naked and acting like I was comfortable.

Not even the countless niggas that stayed trying to holla made me feel like I used to. I used to be confident as hell, back before my parents' died and everything changed.

One nigga came to mind when I thought about my life before and that was the same nigga who first broke my heart. Even before coming to Houston. Thinking of his ass fucked my mood up more than it was.

Sometimes shit changes you and you barely remember who you used to be. It was like I lived as an entirely different person for the first fifteen years of my life compared to the life I lived now.

I brushed my hair through one more time and got my thoughts back focused on finishing getting ready. It was time to get back to reality and the money I was trying to make.

There was no point sitting here thinking about shit that was pointless to think about or old childhood crushes. I was good and would forever be good. Fuck all that shit.

I sighed heavily before adjusting my G-string and pulling the sides up higher to make my hips stand out, making my ass and shape look like I had work done.

I was considered slim thick, but had more ass and titties than the typical skinny girl. I was dark skinned with some red undertones that illuminated my features.

Standing in the full body mirror to the side of where I had been getting ready I had to admit I looked the part. I barely recognized myself with the extra inches the new weave added, the small G-string and tiny ass bra that barely covered my breasts which spilled out on all sides.

Tonight I was gonna be the baddest bitch in the place. Even if I didn't feel like it or never done this shit, I had to have that mindset to pull this shit off.

"You're up next." The stage bouncer said looking in my direction.

I turned around ready to get my set over with. I wasn't scary about shit, but this stripping shit had my nerves fucked up. I couldn't stop my body from trembling, so I tried to play that shit off like it was nothing.

The last thing I wanted was to come off as a weak bitch around all these hating ass hoes. Not one of the other girls even spoke a "hello" to my ass when I first showed up over two hours ago.

The only person who said shit was the manager of the club, Carlos, who came down to show me around and give me the ins and outs of what I was expected to do.

His perverted ass didn't want to keep his hands to himself. I let the shit slide, but no job was gonna keep me from cutting a mothafucka if I needed to. I always kept my blades on me, whether in my mouth or weave, I never left home without them anymore.

I chose to wear all black tonight. My hair was laid with 22 inch extensions that the nigga I was seeing paid for. I usually didn't get my hair or nails done, but the stripper life called for me to look a certain way to make money. So I considered spending the money as a necessary investment and nothing more.

The nigga that I was dealing with was more than happy to hear that I was about to be stripping. Matter of fact, I'm sure his ass was out there right now with his lame ass niggas waiting for me to come out.

I was less and less into Jaquan the more time we spent together. I mean what type of real man wants to show off "his" woman's exposed body to his homeboys. That alone let me know he wasn't shit.

But he was still somebody I had been fuckin' with for a minute so I planned to keep his ass around until that shit ran its course.

The music I was supposed to dance to came on. I stepped out from the back and the bitch who just finished came by me bumping me purposely on the shoulder. That dumb hoe only gave me the courage I needed to keep going. Fuck her hating ass.

As the spotlight shined down on me I strutted as sexy as possible to the center of the small stage and grabbed ahold of the pole. The DJ restarted the song and I dropped down with the beat and started popping my ass.

As I listened to Juicy J and Wale's "bounce it", I pretended I was alone dancing in my room. I started feeling on myself and began to rub my breasts through the barely there fabric, squeezing my nipples.

I undid the strings from the back. I was in a zone, and the shit must have been working because dollar bills started flying in front of me.

Niggas and the few bitches close up were cheering my ass on only hyping me more. All while I kept listening to the music and tuned everybody else out.

After my top fell, I dropped down and got on all fours making sure to keep my ass tooted in the air and my back arched. That shit made the niggas sitting on the side of the stage come closer to the edge just like I wanted.

I started crawling in their direction so I could give their asses a real show. I had planned on playing the side where there was some ballers when I first peeped them in the crowd earlier. The niggas looked like they had a lot of dough, so to me they were my ticket for the night.

When I got to the edge of the stage I turned around so that my pussy was visible through the thong that I was wearing. I spread my legs in a V with them straight in the air and kept moving my body to the rhythm of the song.

After I teased the niggas by rubbing my pussy through the material. I slid it to the side, but just before I could really give the niggas a show I felt myself being pulled up off the stage and flipped over some nigga's shoulder.

I didn't know what the fuck was going on. I didn't even have time to look up and see who the fuck snatched my ass.

I was being kidnapped and nobody was trying to help either. I pounded on the stranger's chest while he had me flipped over his shoulder.

"What the fuck, let me go!" I screamed trying to get him to put me down.

"calm your ass down, damn shawty." He barked at me.

"Let me GO!" I yelled again still punching and kicking, but it was like nothing I was doing phased the man.

His ass kept walking toward the exit of the club like it wasn't shit. I kept kicking and screaming too.

As soon as the door to the outside opened, I felt the cold ass winter air on my almost naked body. Even Houston got cold in the winter for those of us who lived down here.

The cold caused my whole body to shake but I didn't give a fuck about how cold it was. Who the fuck was this nigga? And where the fuck was he taking me?

The nigga that snatched my ass up stopped just outside the front door to the club and set me down.

I was a hundred percent sure I didn't know this nigga. From his build and even his damn cologne I would have remembered his ass, I was sure of that shit.

My instincts were in full effect and all I thought of was running the fuck away and getting the hell away from whoever he was.

Once I fixed my hair enough that it wasn't in my face, I turned to run. But his ass held onto my shoulder from behind to keep me in place.

I finally gave up trying to get away for the time being, and instead turned back around to see who the fuck he was, since he was doing all this shit and it was obvious he wouldn't let me go.

As soon as I got a good look at the man standing in front of me I was ready to get the fuck on and not waste my time out in the cold a second longer. I couldn't believe this shit.

He didn't say shit either. He just stared at my ass with a look I couldn't figure out, before taking his shirt off and trying to hand it to me. I felt the cold but forgot that I was almost naked when I tried to get the fuck away from this nigga.

Now that I knew who it was, I wasn't worried about his ass doing some shit, but I still wanted to get the away. The man in front of me was the last nigga alive I wanted to see, especially at this place.

Instead of taking the shirt he offered or speaking to him, I turned on my heel again and started walking the fuck away. This time he didn't stop me.

The fuck did he think? I was gonna stand out here and talk to his ass?

I couldn't help the few tears that escaped as I picked up my pace trying to go anywhere but out here with him. I crossed my arms over my chest and finally made it over to the side entrance which led to the dressing room.

I hurried up and pulled at the door handle to get my ass inside, but of course shit wasn't working in my favor and his ass caught up to me. He pressed his hand against the door while leaning his body close into mine from behind before I could open the shit a crack.

So I turned back around and mean mugged his ass.

"The fuck you want nigga? Damn!" I yelled letting his ass know my thoughts.

"Come get in the car shawty." He said all calm and in the same deep accent I remembered better than I should.

I thought about trying to get the fuck away from him again or to just ignore his ass. But one thing I knew about Saint was that he never gave in.

Even when we were children he was relentless and stubborn as hell. I already knew there wasn't shit I could do at this point to avoid doing what he said. His ass would probably just pick me up and carry me if I said no.

So instead of saying anything back to his ass I nodded my head in agreement while I kept my arms folded in front of me.

He forcefully took his shirt and put that shit over my head, dressing me like I was a little ass girl.

"You really stubborn ass hell." He said while putting it on me.

I didn't do nothing to help or stop his ass either. I wanted him to realize I wasn't agreeing to get in his car because I wanted to or out of my own free will.

After the shirt was on me, he turned around and grabbed ahold of my hand in a tight ass grasp. I guess to keep my ass from running the fuck away, like I wanted to.

The only thing this nigga had to say that I would be interested in hearing was how his sister, my best friend was doing.

I hadn't spoke to her in ten years. The day of the funeral, the day this nigga fucked up my heart and made me feel worthless, was the last time I saw or spoke to a soul back home. It seemed like a damn lifetime ago.

I reluctantly followed behind Saint, trying to brace myself for the conversation I knew was about to take place. I wasn't the type of bitch to run away when I was confronted, so by the time I slid into the passenger seat of his expensive ass whip I had regained my composure and was prepared to hear whatever the fuck he wanted to talk about.

Saint

10 years was a long fucking time. I could hardly believe that shit was happening the way it was. The last fucking thing I expected to see tonight was Nya's ass up on stage busting her shit open for a crowd of niggas to watch.

Nya was the definition of good girl coming up. She was a tom boy until she finally started getting the body she grew into.

I would have never thought she would be stripping. I didn't even know her ass was out in Houston in the first place.

I was here on some business and out coolin' with my niggas enjoying the nightlife the city had to offer for our last night in town.

The minute she walked on stage I was drawn to her and racked my brain, thinking of how the fuck I knew the damn girl.

Then when she was down in front of those whack ass niggas sitting stage side like the thirsty ass clowns they were, I got a good ass look at her face.

She really didn't change that much over the years. The moment the light shined on her face I realized who the fuck I was looking at, and I instantly took action without a fucking thought.

I left out of the VIP section we were kicked back in and snatched her ass up off the shit. The niggas that worked the club were all some pussies and didn't do shit about it.

Nya should never have been up on the stage in the first place, and I bet any fucking thing she never would be again. I put that shit on everything.

I didn't know shit about shawty's life now, or why the fuck she would do some shit like this. I really didn't know a damn thing about her.

But Nya was my responsibility and that shit hadn't changed no matter how much time passed. She may not know how things were about to change for her, but she was gonna find out.

We sat in the parking lot outside the club in silence for a good ten minutes before I broke the silence that filled my ride.

"How you livin' shawty? This shit ain't meant for you and I ain't fuckin' 'wit it." I said right out.

Letting her know my feelings right away, about her stripping and shit.

I wasn't usually a judgmental nigga. So that was the last thing I was trying to do. But Nya was better than this shit.

"Saint... This my life and my business. You ain't got a say in what I got goin' on. You ain't my daddy or MY nigga. The only reason I agreed to sit here with you was because I know your ass wasn't gonna take "no" for an answer." She responded, rolling her eyes.

I shook my head at the shit she said back to me. I wasn't about to go back and forth with her right now. I caught that last part about being her nigga and heard that shit for what it was. But I wasn't going there with her.

There wasn't a chance in hell she would be stripping again. But what I really wanted to know was how the fuck she ended up here in the first place. After her parents died and she up and left, I tried looking for her and her brother.

I did everything I knew to try and find where the fuck they were at. I was only 17 at the time, but I saw them as my family too.

I was already taking care of my sister and had been holding shit down.

That shit started the day I was old enough to count money, weigh shit out and pull a trigger. I started off hustling in the hood following behind a couple of my older cousins.

By the time I was in high school, I brought in enough bread to handle shit. All I fucking knew was getting money from sunup to sundown.

The only word that got back to me was that her aunt took her and her little brother back to Houston, but it was like nobody knew shit for sure.

I let the shit go after a few months and counted it as a loss. I figured if Nya wanted to reach out she would, but she never even called or no shit. She just up and vanished.

I thought about her ass from time to time, I couldn't even lie. The way shit played out made me think she couldn't handle my rejection on top of losing her parents, so that was why she kept her distance.

My sister was fucked up behind the way shit went down too. She never understood how Nya didn't ever call or no shit. It was always a damn mystery as to what the fuck really happened.

Before she left, her and Jolie were inseparable. We were all family in my eyes. We were all young as hell, but had been around each other for years.

I made it a point to look out for her and she knew that shit. Nya knew what it was and that me and Jolie were her family even if her parents were gone. She would've been straight. None of the shit sat right with me.

"Maybe you forgot, when I say some shit, I mean just what the fuck I say. I'll let that shit slide for now 'cus it's been a long ass time. Now, how the fuck you out here like this shawty, ya heard."

"I'm not out here like this for your information." Nya said getting loud.

Nya always had the worst tempter. She would be all calm and shit, then when a person said something she found disrespectful, that sweet and innocent shit went out the window. A whole other side to lil' baby came out. She would flip the fuck out.

"I seen that shit for myself, busting your pussy open on stage. How the fuck you not out here like that." I said matching her volume.

I guess the shit I said hit home, because she piped the fuck down real quick. The next shit she said was in a lot calmer tone than before.

"So what you wanna know. 'bout the fucked up life I was forced to live, the abuse.. what nigga? That was the shit that was offered to me and Terrell. There's not a damn thing I wouldn't do to keep him from all that. So yeah, if it takes showing some niggas some shit, than that's just what the fuck I'm finin' to do, ya heard." She answered, letting her accent from back home come out more than it was before.

This was Nya. The Nya I knew who was strong as hell and the furthest thing from a weak bitch.

Before her parents got killed, she always stood tall and didn't let her feelings get in the way. The real shit she just told my ass showed me that she really hadn't changed that much over the years.

She wasn't just on stage disrespecting herself because she wanted to, she did that shit because she needed to. Who the fuck could tell her she was wrong for that, when I was out in the streets hustling myself.

I always liked to think shit over before I responded so my bad ass temper wouldn't come out. Whenever that happened mothafuckas lost their lives.

I caught the other shit Nya spoke on about abuse and heard the hurt in her voice. This girl still had a big ass place in my heart even after all this time, whether she knew that shit or not.

I didn't know who the fuck was responsible or what the fuck happened to her along the way that left her to take care of her brother. But when I found out, every person responsible wa gonna get what the fuck they deserved.

For the time being, Nya's answers were enough for me. My goal was to get her back living right and make things better for her and her brother. On top of that, I needed to keep a low profile out here because of the moves I was making. So I would wait and let her tell me all the details when she was ready. Best believe I was gonna handle shit accordingly.

"Okay." I stated simply.

I started up the car and put the shit in drive.

"Where the fuck you tryin' take me nigga?" I gotta get home. I'm not 'bout to be ridin' around with you Saint." She said.

Her tone was calmer than before but she was still uncomfortable being with me. I could tell she was really worried that I wasn't gonna let her go back home at all. I wouldn't do her like that knowing she had Terrell to take care of.

The lil' nigga had to be about grown himself now, probably in high school. Knowing that Nya held shit down and took care of him the way she was, only left me more convinced that she was still the same Nya I knew.

That was some real shit, for a bitch to be able to hold shit down when she didn't have to do it in the first place. She was doing it by herself from the sound of it too.

I knew she was talking about getting home to her brother, but if I hadn't scooped her ass up she would still be in the club working. I decided to just grab something to eat before I took her back.

That way we could spend some more time catching up. Nya was always cool as hell to be around. Even though I hadn't seen her in years it felt good as hell to have her next to me.

I turned up the music and then pulled out my phone. I sent a text to my nigga Buck letting him know that I was dipping out for the rest of the night and would get up with him in the morning before we headed back.

Then I went ahead and hit the send button for my sister's contact. She picked up almost right away and sounded like she had been drinking.

My sister was 25 years old just like Nya and was a school teacher. But on the weekends she stayed in some shit.

She usually went out with some of her hoe ass friends. I always kept tabs on her ass though. That way nothing went down whether I was in town or not.

As long as she stayed local she was good. Too many mothafuckas wanted to stay on my good side for anyone to mess with her.

"Jolie, you ain't gonna believe this shit. Nya next to me." I kept shit short and simple.

My sister was always all extra and talked too much.

I was gonna let Nya do all the talking on this one. I didn't know much about her situation anyway to be giving messages and shit.

So I went ahead and handed the phone over to her. She snatched up the shit out of my hand quick as hell with a smile on her face.

I saw how excited Nya was from the corner of my eye and heard Jolie screaming into the shit. I could hear her damn voice from where I was sitting.

While Nya and her were talking I was able to piece together some more shit from what she was telling my little sister.

I figured shit out enough to know that she was sticking to the basics of what had been her life for the past decade. That was straight for now.

It seemed like her aunt took her to some fucked up living situation and then kept her from contacting anyone for the first year.

After that she gave up trying to get back home and accepted living in Houston. She kept shit vague as hell. But she did tell Jolie that she worked at a doctor's office as a receptionist or some shit.

Knowing that she had been making other moves besides stripping put my mind at ease more about finding her like I did. It was obvious she didn't wanna mention how I found her to Jolie and I would respect her in that.

After they hung up, Nya handed me back my phone.

"Thanks." She said quietly.

That was the end of our conversation for the rest of the ride. While she was on the phone I came up with my next move too. I pulled into a Denys parking lot and then parked the ride.

"We gonna grab somethin' to eat then I'm gonna say what I got to say" I told her before she could question me.

I knew she would ask why we were here and all that other shit. But I wasn't going for it right now. She went ahead and got out of the whip right after I did and walked by my side into the restaurant.

I forgot she didn't really have shit on. She was still wearing her high ass stripper heals and the shirt I gave her. At least that went down to her mid-thigh. So her body wasn't exposed too much.

The place was packed since it was just after all the clubs let out. Most of the heads were turning because Nya was sexy as fuck.

She looked like a queen no matter what the fuck she wore. The bitches were turning their heads in my direction but I wasn't paying none of the hoes attention. Nya was my only priority right now.

I let her lead the way. She walked over to the table near that back. The last time I saw Nya we were still young as fuck. The years hadn't done nothing but make her ass fatter and body develop even more.

Walking behind her my eyes fell right to her ass and the sway of her thick hips. Nya was slim thick but her ass was definitely more on the thick side. She was built for her size.

Before she sat down I looked back up and played shit off like I wasn't watching her the way I was. This was the same way shit was for me back in the day too. She was always on the sister tip to me and I had no plans of that shit changing even now that we were grown.

After we sat down, the waitress came and got our drink orders. I leaned back in the booth, looking over the menu.

"After we eat, can you just take me back to the club. I need to get my car and shit so I can go back home." Nya asked.

I chose to ignore her and waited all the way until after we got our drinks and made our orders to say anything back.

I was gonna lay shit out there and tell her the shit that was on my mind.

"You really tryin' to stay out here, or you wanna come back home? You don't belong here. You need to come back and make shit happen the right way. You know me and sis got your back and gonna make sure you straight shawty."

She didn't respond, but I could tell she was in deep thought about the shit I just said. Nya and me were a lot alike when it came to thinking shit over before reacting. We were a lot alike in other ways too. Just like our tempers.

Our food was brought to us and she must have been as hungry as me because we both tore into our plates.

We started reminiscing about the one time Nya and Jolie schooled some niggas in a street basketball game. The niggas tried calling her ugly, until her and my sister beat their asses, throwing them hands on them like I taught them.

We were laughing, recalling how they ran off like the little bitches they were, when we were interrupted by a couple of niggas who made it their business to step to our table.

I instantly moved my hand to my piece at my back. I wasn't back home, and I didn't have my niggas with me. But I would never be a bitch. If some shit popped off, it was gonna be what it was gonna be.

I really wasn't feeling the way ol' boy was looking at Nya. I knew from the jump that the nigga was a fucking bitch.

NyAsia (Nya)

I was actually starting to loosen up a little for the first time in what seemed like forever. Matter of fact it seemed like the first time I could really breathe again since moving to Houston.

That shit might not make any sense since I was now grown and could go and do anything I pleased. But being in Saint's presence had me feeling like the real me. Like the me before the terrible shit happened.

The me, that I was meant to be, but couldn't be because life went a different route. It felt good as hell to sit back and not be stressed the fuck out or be on guard around whoever I was with.

Even when I dated a nigga or hung out with bitches out here, it was never the same as it was before. Saint knew the real me.

Remembering the time me and Jolie whooped them boys' ass for calling us ugly when we beat them in a game, had us both about rolling on the floor.

That was until Jaquan came up trying to start some shit.

I knew the minute his ass stepped to the table from the look in his eyes that it was gonna be some shit. Jaquan wasn't my man even though he tried to play like I was his bitch.

I always made it clear that I didn't want a relationship, but for whatever reason he kept on with the clingy shit. It didn't even make sense since he had other bitches he was fucking around with that I knew about.

He would try and throw them in my face, but I really didn't give a fuck about his ass to be worried about what he was into. I never let him hit raw and made sure that there was no slip ups. When it came to my health I didn't play, even for some decent dick.

"Ayo, what the fuck you doing NyAsia?" He asked trying to come off hard.

"None of your business nigga." I said calmly back.

I really wasn't trying to let this nigga cause a seen, because it would all be for nothing. We weren't together, so he had absolutely no reason to be questioning me. I guess Jaquan wasn't feeling my answer.

The thing was, he never tried to check me when we saw each other in public. If I was out, I danced and talked to who I wanted to.

Him acting all possessive tonight was something new. Yeah he always tried to convince me to be his woman and talked shit about the niggas I talked to behind closed doors when we were alone. But he never acted like he was acting now.

He was feeling real bold because he reached down and grabbed ahold of my arm rough as hell trying to pull me up. I wasn't having that shit and I pulled my arm right back, avoiding his attempt at getting me up out the booth seat.

I sat there in a stare off with him for a split second giving him a look that dared him to try that shit again. I would split the mothafucka's hand if he reached out to grab me again. That one attempt was enough for Saint though.

He hopped up and had his piece out pressed up against Jaquan's temple in the next moment.

That was another thing about Saint, he always looked out for me like the way he was doing now. I wasn't surprised because this same scene had played out a few times back home when we were a lot younger.

That's where he got his nickname from. Me and Jolie always used to tease him calling him our "Saint" because he protected us. At first he tried to say that nickname made him sound like a bitch, but we kept on, until the whole hood used it.

After time passed, the nickname stuck and he didn't worry about how it made him sound anymore, because he had put in so much work in the streets that there wasn't a doubt about how he got down. By that time, nobody dared to call him by his real name.

Saint looked Jaquan dead in the eyes and stayed calm even when the waitress came back and screamed causing the whole damn restaurant to start wilding out running out of the place.

I knew for a fact that 12 was about to be here any minute.

"I'll die behind this one nigga. Will you?" Saint said in his normal toned voice without a trace of feeling in it and pressing the gun harder into the side of Jaquan's head.

Jaquan shook his head no and kept his mouth closed.

"Get the fuck on mothafucka." He lowered his weapon and gestured for Jaquan to head out by waving the tool in the direction of the entrance to the restaurant.

His ass turned around and started walking off with his niggas right beside him. Him and his boys could be heard mumbling shit as they made their way out the door.

We heard sirens approaching from the distance and got the fuck on. Saint laid a few hundreds on the table and put his finger to his lips while looking over at the waitress on our way out.

We made it out of the parking lot just before the police arrived.

He wasn't from here, so the chances of them pinning anything on him were slim. There was a lot of crime in this area of the city so the police would probably just figure it was some local beef instead of someone from out of town.

I didn't say shit the whole ride and waited until Saint spoke up again. We were all the way back over by the club where my car was parked.

"That's the type of niggas you fuckin' with. You gotta watch the company you keep baby." He said.

"Whatever, it's not like that." I said keeping details to a minimum. I waved off his shit talking.

"But for real, I'm leaving' in the morning and I meant the shit I said. I'll give you a few days but then I'm coming to get your ass, if you don't get up with me and make shit happen." Saint said all serious again.

"We gon' act like you didn't just do that shit back there? Like, that's not normal Saint, and my life believe it or not, is drama free for the first time in a long time finally. I'm not trying to lose that." I responded to his demand of me moving back home.

I was serious as hell too. Over the last year, life for me and Terrell had finally settled in to a comfortable routine. I had a decent job as a receptionist and didn't wanna go backwards by moving back home and having nothing again.

I had been at square one for nine years struggling. I really couldn't see me leaving my life here. It wasn't great by no means, but it was something and I had fought hard for the little bit of shit I did have.

"You and Terrell don't belong out here." He said back like he didn't hear a word I just said.

"Whatever!" I huffed and gave up trying to talk sense into him.

When Saint didn't wanna hear some shit, he pretended like he didn't. To me he was always childish that way. He always had to have his way.

But this time I was serious. He would just find that shit out the hard way, when I didn't get up with him or agree to move back to New Orleans.

After he pulled up next to my car, I hurried my ass on and tried to get out his ride fast as hell to avoid any more of the conversation I wasn't trying to have.

"I'ma wait out here 'til you get your shit, then I need you to bring your phone over here so I can make sure you don't try to run away again." He said with a smile on his face easing his way back to the subject again.

Yeah, the nigga wasn't letting up.

I sighed and then opened the door. I did like he said and after going inside the club and grabbing my shit, I stepped back over to his car and handed over my phone.

After asking for my passcode, which was just a box sequence, he used it to call his phone. That way he could save my number.

He handed it back over to me through the window and then gave me one of the looks I had missed all these years.

Saint always tried to play it off like he wasn't attracted to me, but he couldn't help but look my body over with the desire showing all over his face. I was older now and even more confident that the look he always gave was in fact one of attraction.

When we were younger, I always thought he might be into me. I used to sit up thinking about what it would be like to even kiss him, I mean really being together. Little girl fantasies and shit. But then his ass shut me down when I tried taking it there.

I smirked at his ass and met his gaze when his eyes made it back to my face.

"I see you nigga." I said leaving the rest of what I was thinking out of the conversation.

"Good seeing you too Nya. Im'a follow you home and make sure you're straight before I head out." He said in response.

I nodded my head and then walked my ass right back over to my ride. My shit was nothing special but it was my first car ever and I was proud of it. Even if it was an old ass Buick. The shit worked and it was all mine.

I knew Saint was watching and felt his eyes burning a hole in me, but I didn't turn around. It was still fuck Saint as far as I was concerned.

Saint

Even though last night was fucked up finding Nya's ass stripping, I was still glad that I ran into her. To me that shit alone was a sign that she wasn't meant for the life she was living. Hell I knew that shit without a damn sign.

This morning I woke up early as fuck. Usually I would've been knee deep in pussy with one of the local bitches I fucked with when I came out this way. But that shit didn't happen last night with me being occupied with Nya.

I didn't want love, but pussy was something completely different. I was used to fucking daily to keep my head clear.

The bitches I fucked with knew what it was and didn't give me too many problems since I always laid shit out there for them and told them I was only looking to fuck. If they were on bullshit, I didn't deal with the hoe at all.

I sat up in bed and adjusted my hard dick before picking up my phone and turning the shit back on. I kept my main cell off at night. Only legit mothafuckas had my main line besides Buck, Jolie and now Nya.

I kept my work phone on vibrate and my burner cell that I changed out every month was only on when shipments were in transport or being delivered.

I picked up my work phone and dialed Martina's number. I didn't store any numbers in my work phone and erased all calls in case I was ever picked up by the boys. They weren't getting shit out of me.

I climbed to the top of my city because of everything I picked up in the pen. I only served 12 months, but that little ass bid proved to be useful as hell.

It was my second felony charge for possession with intent and a firearm charge. I was moving reckless as hell before.

But while I was inside I spent a lot of fucking time getting my mind right and the shit made me come out a beast. My whole attitude and ambition changed.

I was on to bigger and better shit all the way around. I lived with the reality that tomorrow wasn't promised and I could get hit with life sentences if I got caught up with the shit I was doing now.

That kept me changing shit up and trying to plan things out to stay 10 steps ahead at all times.

When Martina answered on the other line, I got straight to the reason I called her ass. I let her know shit went off without a problem and my team was moving forward.

Mc and my niggas came out here and put in some work for the plug. Now that his problem was taken care of it meant my team was free to take over the territory of the niggas we handled.

I was part of some real organized crime shit back in New Orleans. A few years back me and a few other bosses in the city came together to form an organization known as the Three C's, short for "Choppa City Cartel".

We were all supplied by the same connect, so us coming together helped to keep us all on top without outside competitors coming in trying to undercut our shit.

So far it proved smart as hell for all three of our teams. We were all getting money and eating good.

There were differences in how each of our teams ran shit. Each boss had complete control over their crew. As long as they kept to our agreement of prices and territory there was no problems.

My team was the fucking truth and in my opinion a cut above the others across the city. We didn't have no inside beef and shit ran like a business. It helped that I looked out for all the niggas on my team. I made sure they had enough dough to stay laced and their pockets were filled as long as they kept putting in work.

Everybody under me got their fair share and the shit was solid as hell for the past couple of years.

Buck was my right hand. He was my mothafuckin' partna. Me and him were best friends coming up and that shit hadn't changed after all these years. In my eyes he was my equal and just as much the boss of this shit.

But I handled all the business and to everyone else they looked to me as the leader. That was only because Buck didn't have patience for the shit and didn't want to talk to the niggas on our team more than he had to.

He was antisocial as fuck. It was better that way anyway because he was a stone cold killer. When he felt disrespected he didn't talk about the shit, he just laid niggas out.

Everyone always thought he was off in the head, and the shit was partially true. He had it even worse than me coming up and was bounced around to a few foster homes, before I finally got my granddaddy to let him stay with us.

All it took was me paying him a few bands to keep him happy each month. I was nine years old when I started hustling and paying rent and shit.

My grandfather wasn't shit either. At least he let us live with him I guess, but he was a greedy and heartless ass nigga. He never gave a fuck about me and couldn't stand Jolie.

I got his ass to shut that dumb shit up he always spouted off at her, when I finally showed him who the fuck I was. I remember that day like it was yesterday.

He kept yelling and screaming all kinds of shit at my sister. Calling her out her name talking to her like she wasn't shit. My sister was a combination of who knows what and looked light as hell.

Most people thought she could pass for white, but she had a few features from our father.

Our grandfather always took out his anger on her and would beat her worse than me, even when she didn't do shit to deserve it.

I was the one who always got into shit, Jolie was quiet when we were home. She never wanted to say the wrong shit to set his ass off. Normally she was outgoing and had one of the biggest mouths I knew.

I was tired of listening to him call her a "lil bitch", "no good", dumb" all that shit he always said.

The last straw was when he went in her room with his belt in his hand and told her to bend over. Jolie literally just got home from school. We both did, and she didn't even have time to do nothing to piss the mothafucka off.

I came in behind him with my pistol in my hand and got his attention real quick,

"You ain't doin' shit to MY sister!" I yelled at him while cocking the gun.

His ass turned around and at first he looked skeptical that I was really gonna do shit. So I looked his ass in the eye.

"Try it and see what the fuck happen." I said with steel in my voice. I may have only been 9 years old but I wasn't scared of shit.

He must have heard how serious I was and saw the look in my eye. The nigga would be dead if he touched my sister again. I meant that shit with all my heart.

That was the day that I really became the man I was. I handled mine and no nigga alive put fear in my heart. From that day on, our grandfather didn't' say shit to either of us.

He collected the money I left on the counter for his ass each month on the first and barely came back to the house otherwise. I was glad as hell because that nigga wasn't family to me.

Jolie, Nya and Buck were my only family out here.

Buck was a fucking brother to me. When I was inside he looked out and kept money on my books. I did the same shit for him when he got popped a few months after I got out.

Now we were moving smarter and trying to do shit right and avoid dumb mistakes that would lead us right back behind them bars.

Next in line was Smoke. He was solid as fuck, working his way up. He moved out to New Orleans right after Nya's ass disappeared.

Even though we hadn't come up together he gained my trust over the years of putting in work without shit going wrong.

He proved to be loyal when he took out a nigga that came at me without hesitating. It was hard to come by a loyal shooter and I wanted a nigga like him close by for when shit popped off. His ass was promoted and now he was in charge of two of our traps.

We had a total of 4 spots all on the West Bank.

The other bosses kept their shit in their hoods too. One was Downtown and the other was Uptown. The only problems our organization had going on was some shit in the 3rd ward.

The beef between the YMM's and 110'ers had boiled over a while back. But that shit really didn't affect the work going on over on this side of town. My money was still stacking and looking right.

Matter of fact our bread was more than just stacking. That was why I was ready to expand to Houston. It was time to build this shit up. Right now our traps kept meth, cocaine, heroin, pills and syrup in them.

Me and Buck didn't touch none of the shit personally and never broke shit down anymore. Those days were over as soon as we set up our own shop. We had niggas in charge of the traps and they made the decisions of who was in charge of doing what.

We dealt with shit on a wholesale level and made sure numbers added up. If some shit came up short then we dealt with it personally. We were only shorted one time in the past three years.

Shit was smooth sailing and at the top we were bringing in a $200,000 profit from our heroine and coke each month. That didn't even include the other shit that we supplied.

Prices were set to make the most profit but also the same as the other teams in the city on the street level. All of us bosses were getting our weight for the same prices from the plug too. I was content with the shit, but I was ready to make more money plain and simple.

In this game there was no such thing as too much money or too much power. Buck was hesitant about the changes that were gonna need to happen, but he was with the shit once I ran the projected numbers by him. Mothafuckas aren't gonna turn down a chance to triple their dough.

With the expansion we would each bring in an additional million in profit a month and then split that shit down the middle. The territory in Houston we were taking over was bigger than our shit here in the West Bank. I was cool with that since doing too much shit close to home was never good.

At the same time, I was still trying to figure out how to handle everything and whether I was moving to Houston full time or not. Buck planned on staying in town. He wasn't trying to go no damn where.

His ass always got uneasy when he was away from the hood for too long. He was a certified gangsta and didn't like trying to fit in out in public or in new cities and shit.

After I told Martina everything was good, she tried to stay on the phone. She asked if I was gonna stop through when I got back in town.

That was a whole other situation I had on my plate right now. I had been fucking the plug's daughter since before we even started doing business together. He didn't have a clue about the shit we had going on.

What had me more fucked, was Martina switched up. She went from being cool with fucking and no strings to acting all crazy.

She started calling more and begging for the dick daily. I wasn't trying to wife no bitch and definitely not the plug's daughter. I came through and laid the dick on her when I was in need of some pussy and that was it.

She even went as far as trying to pillow talk and try to convince me to make shit official with her. When she brought that shit up and talked about me asking her father's permission and shit I knew that it was time to put an end to us fucking around. No pussy was worth dying for and her pussy wasn't even all that.

I didn't think I would ever have feelings for a bitch outside Jolie and Nya. My parents fucked up my view on love so that no bitch stood a damn chance.

I never even did the girlfriend shit. Martina and all the other delusional bitches were out of their minds if they thought otherwise.

"When are you coming over to see me, papi?" Martina cooed into the phone.

"You gotta stop buggin' yo." I answered. Just hearing her ask when I was coming to see her, started stressing me the fuck out.

"But my panocha mojada." She said sounding sexy as fuck.

I didn't speak much Spanish, but I understood the few words she just said. She was telling me that her "pussy was wet".

"I got you, I'll be there later. Keep it wet for me." I responded, then hung up the phone.

I would stop through Martina's spot when I made it back despite the extra shit she was doing. She was an all-out freak. She let me do whatever the fuck I wanted with her.

I needed to release some built up tension anyway. But the real fucking reason was to keep shawty happy until I was ready to make the move to end shit for good.

I needed to find a way to stop fucking with her without it costing me my life or fucking up business. Martina's hoe ass might have had the upper hand right now, but that shit wasn't gonna last long. I already had shit in motion to fix it.

After I showered and got dressed, I hit Buck up. It was time to get the fuck up out of Houston and head back home.

We met down in the lobby a few minutes later. Smoke wasn't with Buck when he came down. It was typical of his ass to show up a few minutes later.

Smoke had his shades on and walked at a slow ass pace. He was wild as fuck so there was no telling what he got into after the strip club last night. His ass was probably up all night.

Smoke was the type of nigga that didn't give a fuck. He did what the fuck he wanted without thinking twice. Shit was always coming back on him for his reckless decisions and shit, but as long as it didn't affect my business I didn't give a fuck what the nigga did on his personal time.

All three of us were cool. But Buck was skeptical of Smoke even after all these years. He only spoke on the shit a few times when he witnessed some of the shit Smoke had going on first hand.

But even he agreed that as long as it didn't interfere with business than the shit didn't matter. The day that shit changed and his reckless attitude got mixed up in the shit we had going on, then we would take care of it.

"Let's head out." I said after greeting each of my niggas.

"Hell yeah, I need to get back, that hoe's pussy was whack as fuck." Smoke said all loud looking over in the direction where some young looking girl was strutting past in some little ass dress I'm sure was from last night.

"These Houston thots ain't nothing like what we got back home."

The bitch heard his ass and gave him an evil ass look. She started to come back over in our direction, but luckily she saw Buck shake his head no.

He was a nigga that put fear in just about everybody. So I wasn't surprised when the bitch turned back around and walked out the way she was headed before Smoke talked shit.

That girl looked like a lil' juvie barely 18. Smoke better be careful about that jailbait shit. Otherwise his ass would end up locked up behind some young pussy. That charge was some shit you didn't want behind them bars.

People in the hotel lobby looked on but didn't say shit. Me and Buck were used to all the shit Smoke did and said. It didn't matter where we were that nigga didn't give a fuck. I never took his ass anywhere important for that reason alone. He was dependable when it came to handling shit in the streets, but his ass was never gonna sit down and meet the plug because he would be dead before the shit even started.

Me and Buck carried ourselves different. We didn't like to draw too much attention to ourselves. Smoke was who he was and we had grown accustomed to the shit. If the hit would have needed more discretion then his ass wouldn't have even come along.

He didn't know all the details of our operation and that was how we were gonna keep it. We trusted him like we trusted the rest of our team, just enough to get shit done but still look at them as a threat.

Buck was the only nigga I counted on to have my back when some real shit came our way. The code was to get it by any means after all and mothafuckas were capable of anything.

We headed out of the hotel and got in my car. Last night we copped a rental to make the moves that we did, but Buck dropped that shit back off early this morning. After fueling up and grabbing some food we hit I-10 and headed back. I turned the music up to listen to my shit.

I wasn't a nigga to sit up and talk while I rode. Driving was where I did most of my thinking. All I kept thinking about was Nya's sexy ass though.

Last night when I got back to my room I couldn't stop thinking about her ass either. Shit was like old times, but now we were both older.

I couldn't get over how much she still affected me after all this time. Her body was crazy. She was stacked with nice size titties that still sat up without a bra. When she was on stage popping her ass, I imagined what it would be like to hit it from the back.

The problem was, Nya wasn't meant to show off her body to a room full of niggas. I still wasn't over that shit. I was just glad that I stopped her from going all out and letting them bitch ass niggas see her pussy up close.

Seeing her like that first hand was gonna be imprinted in my fucking brain. I would never be able to look at her ass without thinking about fucking and I wasn't trying to go there with her no matter what.

But shit, shawty's body was bad as fuck. Everything from her dark skin, hips, ass and smile drew me in. It was the same when we were kids. It was like I was her nigga but I wasn't.

I meant what the fuck I said too, she better not try playing with my ass. That fuck nigga too. I couldn't believe she let some clown like that in her life. She was really out here down bad.

But now she was about to come right back up, since me and Jolie were back in her life. She had two days and then I was coming back for her ass whether she liked that shit or not.

We made it back home in three and a half hours. The drive usually takes most mothafuckas five but I was trying to get the fuck back to keep the heat off us.

After we got across the bridge to our hood, on the west bank, I went ahead and dropped both Smoke and Buck off.

Smoke's ass was hard as fuck to wake up. Since he was passed out in the backseat of my Range I had to shake him for a few minutes, but he finally woke the fuck up.

It was just after noon and Martina was still hitting me up back to back for the last hour. I looked down at my phone and opened up the last few messages she sent. There was a picture of her laid out on her bed playing in her pussy.

It was definitely time for me to head her way. I drove back across the bridge and was downtown in the Garden District in no time.

I pulled into her round about drive way that led to her big ass house. This was the real uppity ass neighborhood in New Orleans.

I didn't have a fucking clue why Martina wanted to be right in the middle of this shit. In my opinion, being this close to politicians and judges would make me feel like a target.

But I guess growing up as the princess of a cartel makes you think different than a nigga like me.

I came up out the mud so all this shit wasn't me. I was paranoid as fuck. As my money got longer, that shit only got worse. I didn't think I would ever move to a neighborhood like this shit here.

I parked right in front of the granite steps and wasted no time getting out. I walked up to the door and stopped ready to knock, but didn't get a damn chance before Martina opened the shit. This bitch was ready to fuck.

Martina was a fine ass Spanish bitch. She was more of the model type and didn't have as much ass or titties as the bitches I usually fucked with. But her pussy stayed wet and tight, and she let me do whatever the fuck I wanted in the bedroom.

She didn't fuck with any other street niggas that I knew of either. I didn't give a fuck who she messed with, but I never wanted another nigga to come at me because of his bitch. Especially when I didn't give a fuck about none of them past an occasional fuck.

The most a bitch got out of me was some dick and if she was worthy, she might get her pussy ate. I liked all that kinky shit and loved to please a woman.

When I was done with each and every one of them, it was always like none of them had dick before me, by how they acted.

I never met a woman yet that could handle what I was giving them and definitely none that made me reconsider my pledge to never wife one.

Martina leaned in, wrapping one arm around my shoulder and slid her other manicured hand down my pants. She found what she was looking for and instantly gripped my dick with a smile on her face.

I was hard the minute I looked at her standing in nothing but a robe. I knew her ass didn't have shit on underneath the white silk robe she was wearing.

This was the type of shit I liked about her. She stayed ready and waiting for a nigga.

I took a step inside the door while she stroked my dick harder, not letting up. I was already hard, but when she started jacking my dick my shit got even bigger.

Martina began kissing and sucking on my neck. I stood there letting her take the lead for now. She began to work her way down my collarbone and I pushed her head down the rest of the way.

She dropped to her knees right where we stood in the entryway. She didn't even let me get inside good before she had my dick out, so she could handle business and suck my dick here too.

After two days without pussy I was ready for a release. Martina unbuckled my pants and brought my dick to her lips. She tried playing with the tip only sucking on it and shit, but I wasn't here for that teasing shit. She wanted it, so she was gonna eat the mothafucka.

I held her hair back with one hand and grabbed the back of her neck with the other. I pushed her face forward and made her take the dick. She opened her jaws wide and slid her warm wet mouth all the way down the length of my dick.

She couldn't deep throat my shit without choking, but that didn't stop her from trying while she continued to use her tongue the best she could, circling it around.

More spit coated my dick and she moved her mouth faster bobbing her head up and down.

Martina choked and gagged every time I pushed the back of her head making my dick hit her fucking tonsils. So I let my grip go, and the bitch really went to work since she couldn't deep throat my shit.

She picked up the pace, sucking and slurping making a humming noise. Then she slowed down and looked up at me, jacking my dick while using her jaws to suction the top half of my shit.

Looking down at a sexy ass bitch sucking my dick always made me feel like a mothafuckin' king. I loved a woman that wanted to please.

My shit was bigger than most bitches could handle. They struggled fitting it in their mouth and pussy. Martina was no different.

She had sucked my dick plenty of times, but still couldn't fully adjust her mouth. She never made me cum from giving me brain.

I wanted to bust and then bounce. So I went ahead and stepped back and took the rest of my clothes off. I pulled my shirt over my head, leaving only my gold chains on. Martina stood up and untied her robe letting that shit fall to the floor.

I ran my hand over her sexy exposed body causing her to shake under my touch. I wasn't trying to go there with Martina right now. I was here to fuck nothing more and nothing less.

"Take your ass over on them steps." I said and then slapped her on the ass. She took her ass over to the all-white marble staircase that wrapped around the main foyer up to the next floor.

I followed behind her and as soon as her feet were at the bottom of the first step, she stopped. I gripped her ass from behind spreading her wide.

I pressed down on her back and she assumed the position with her hands planted on the steps in front of her. Face down ass up was exactly how she was gonna get the dick today.

"you leakin' girl." I told her as I worked two fingers in and out of her pussy. She was already dripping wet ready for me.

"Yes, papi." She responded in her broken English.

I used my other hand to open her pussy wider and finger fucked her some more until she was bucking back against my hand.

"Keep still shawty." I demanded.

If I was trying to really get into shit, I would've took my time and turned this bitch out. But the more I fucked with Martina the more of a rush I was in. I just wanted to hurry the fuck up and bust this nut.

I moved back and grabbed ahold of her hips, then slid my dick in all the way to the base against the pressure of her tight ass walls.

I was as far as I could go, but my dick still didn't fit all the way so I pulled her body back into me more, really fucking her up.

Martina screamed out back to back, saying all types of shit in Spanish while I continued to move in and out of her.

I dug deeper in them guts going harder and faster while I watched her ass slam against my pelvis.

She tensed up and tried to stop moving altogether but I kept up the pace digging her out. Her juices gushed out, leaving her body limp after her orgasm. I had to hold onto her to keep her up.

So I slowed down and reached one arm forward to grab the back of her neck. I gripped that shit and pulled back enough to bring her head up. That shit made her back arch and ass toot in the air more.

At the same time her pussy clamped the fuck down on my dick. I went harder, fucking the shit outa shawty. Giving her strokes back to back. All that could be heard was slapping and screaming from the way I was beating the pussy up.

"Throw that shit back." I told her.

"No puedo.... Ahhh... lo siento, fuck!" She let out between moans.

"You can't?!" I questioned and stated at the same time. I mean damn she wanted me to come over so bad, and now she was trying to tap out.

She wasn't throwing her shit back at me at all. So I eased up and released the grip I had on her neck. She fell back into the position we started in, with her hands planted in front of her and her head down. It was my turn to take charge and help her do her job.

I reached around and pinched her clit with my hand and grabbed one of her titties with the other.

Martina yelled out, "I can't papi, no mas!"

I slowed down to let her recover. But all that shit she was talking went out the window the minute I did. As soon as I let up she was back rotating her hips trying to get more of the dick.

"Fuck me Saint!"

Her bipolar ass didn't have to tell me twice. I went back to work, fucking her with no mercy. With each stroke I rammed my dick in deeper touching her fucking stomach making the bitch scream.

Her body tensed up and her walls clenched down. Her pussy was leaking and her body was shaking. I laid the dick on her nice and slow with a few more pumps.

That caused her to explode again and squirt all over my dick.

I went ahead and pulled out, busting on her ass with her still bent over in the same position.

It felt good as fuck to get that release, but her pussy didn't leave my legs weak like it should've. Any nigga fucking while standing up felt weak ass knees after busting. But Martina wasn't doing shit for me. Now I was just ready to get the fuck on.

I backed up to where my clothes were on the floor and started putting them back on. I didn't do that laying up shit and wasn't about to start with Martina.

From that garbage pussy and whack ass head I was done fucking with her too. She couldn't suck my dick for shit or fuck me either. Her pussy was wet, tight and she stayed cumming, but me busting was getting harder and harder.

It was time for me to cut ties when it came to this shit.

"Where are you going?" Martina asked starting to get a higher pitched voice, letting her emotions show.

"Saint!... I asked you a fucking question!" She raised her voice another octave coming at me like I was some kind of fucking do-boy.

Martina getting emotional behind my dick was nothing new. She started the shit a while back. This was the first time she came at me with that fucking attitude though and it would be the last.

She was only involved in the drug game by default, since she was born into a cartel family. Her ass shouldn't be involved in none of the shit. She was a weak link and never put in real work a day in her life.

She thought making phone calls was all it took to hold power in this business. But this bitch didn't hold any power over me and I damn sure didn't respect her. I never understood why her father involved her in a damn thing.

Here she was worried about me, a nigga who didn't give a fuck about her. When she should have been focused on the shit that took place in Houston.

All I told her was, it was handled and she was content with that shit. I could have been lying my ass off, but she was more worried about when she was gonna get some dick.

It wasn't my place to help the bitch handle business. Her fuck ups didn't mean shit to me. Now her asking where I was going was just a stupid ass question. I never told her shit about the moves I made.

Me and this bitch never held a conversation outside of basics with shipments and drop-offs. Even the first time we fucked it was on some jump off shit. I met her ass and fucked her in a bathroom with no conversation needed, less than 15 minutes later.

Nothing more than "What's up baby"" was what it took to feel the pussy. So her acting like there was something more between us didn't make sense. Instead of responding to the shit she asked I chose to ignore her altogether.

"I'm out shawty. Get up with me later in the week." I said trying to brush the shit off.

Of course that wasn't happening. I swear this bitch was fucking crazy. She started all out crying, her whole body shaking, like some mental patient, while she wrapped her arms around herself. Sitting butt ass naked on the steps and all.

I didn't know what to do for her and I wasn't a nigga to comfort a damn soul, let alone some bitch I was fucking that didn't mean shit to me. I just didn't have that shit in me. My heart was cold.

I put on the rest of my clothes and then tried to calm her down as much as I was capable of.

"Don't take shit personally. I gotta bounce." I said in a nicer tone at least.

I wasn't trying to give her ass a reason to send her father after me before I planned shit out. I went to where she was sitting and patted her on the shoulder before turning back around and leaving, closing the door that was still open behind me.

As soon as I closed the door and was out of the house I couldn't do nothing but shake my head at myself. This was definitely the last time I was fucking Martina. This shit just kept getting worse. There was no point in stringing her crazy ass along.

Pussy was nothing to a nigga like me. First thing in the morning, I was figuring out how to get myself out of this shit once and for all.

I hopped back in my whip and looked at my phone. I had three missed calls and a new text.

When I unlocked it and saw they were all from Nya I got real fucking uneasy about the shit. No matter how much time passed I knew the real Nya and it was completely out of character for her to reach out to me like this.

When I told her that she was coming back home for good I already knew she was gonna put up a fight about the shit. Nya never just went along with a damn thing because she was told to. She was stubborn as hell, not as bad as me, but still hard headed as fuck.

That's how I knew her ass would end up back home. I planned on having to go back out to Houston in a couple of days to scoop her and lil' bruh up. I wasn't giving her a choice. The few days I gave her were for her to tie up loose ends.

I hurried up and read the one message she sent. Just that quick, I needed to get the fuck back to Houston. I was on ten, ready to kill this nigga before the end of the day.

I did a U-turn, and got right back on I-10 headed to Houston. Fuck the drive, Nya needed me and from the moment I found her that shit was a done deal. As long as I had breath in my body she would never hurt or go without again.

Nya

It hadn't even been a whole damn day and the effects of me running back into my past was fucking with the little bit of happiness I had managed to have in my life.

Jaquan was all out humiliated last night when Saint pulled that gun on him. But shit, Jaquan was the bitch ass nigga that played himself in the first place.

Now his ass was on that get back shit. He already made his move and it was check mate for me.

This morning my little brother left to get up with some his friends and he never came back when he was supposed to. Terrell never ever, not even once went against something I said.

He always was where I told him to be at the time I told him. So I immediately knew some shit was off.

He was sixteen but he was a good ass kid. He wasn't into the streets or any illegal shit. I made sure he stayed on the right path despite the shit I had to go through. He really didn't know the half. I shielded him from everything the best I could.

The worst shit he had ever been exposed to was walking in when one of the old ass niggas my auntie sent over was getting back dressed after having his way with me.

He was only 8 at the time, but seeing the man in my room caused him to try and protect me. Terrell immediately went into action despite only being half the man's size, trying to take up for me.

He came in swinging attempting to do some damage to the way too old nigga. He was no match for a man that was two times his size.

After that shit happened, I moved out of my aunt's house and made the decision to try and make it on my own. A lot of other shit happened along the way, but every single fucking thing I did was for Terrell from that day on.

I left that house because I didn't want him to see some shit like that ever again. He was still innocent and I wanted to keep it that way. Who knew what the fuck my aunt might do to him. I wasn't taking no chances with that shit.

She proved to be the worst type of human being. That was when I really took on the full responsibility of raising my brother.

After waiting around and Terrell still not being home, I ended up trying to figure out my next move and how to find my little brother. Just sitting in my small ass apartment had me about to go fucking crazy.

I didn't even have any Kush to smoke to calm me the hell down.

It was 3 o'clock and Terrell was two hours late coming home. The shit was all the way off. I didn't have one single fucking person to call that was worth a damn thing or who would give a fuck about Terrell being gone.

The only person I had in my life who might be of some use was Jaquan so I reluctantly called his ass. I figured he was still probably salty about how shit played out last night, but I really didn't have time for him to be all in his feelings.

Hopefully, I would be able to sweet talk the nigga like usual. He was always putty in my hands and I usually could get whatever I wanted out of him. He was weak behind me. He answered almost right away.

"Sup, what you want girl?" He asked in a tone that sounded like he was bothered with me calling his ass.

I usually would read his ass for that shit, but I really needed to try and get his help to find Terrell.

"You know I'm sorry 'bout last night." I said trying to get back on his good side.

"You mean that punk ass nigga you fuckin? I'on give a fuck about that bitch ass nigga." He said, but his anger still seeped through even as he tried to play it off.

"I'm so sorry about that. You know how things are between us... but seeing you last night made me realize how much you mean to me." I was laying it on thick.

I decided to go ahead and see if he would help me look for Terrell or at least get the word out for me.

Jaquan was kind of a big hustler around town and had enough pull to find him if some shit was foul.

He didn't say anything back, so I continued with my fake apoloy, "You're right about him, about everything and I understand if you don't want nothing to do with me because of the shit, but I hope we can still be friends." I said pausing before I kept on with the conversation. "But right now, I need your help. I was hoping you could help me find my brother. I know I fucked up, but you know how I feel about you bae. He's missing and I don't know where to even start looking for him." I said as sweetly as I could.

"It's all good. I got you. Matter of fact he over here right now. He's got some business to handle then he'll be home. Since you got some making up to do, how 'bout I just bring him back with me when I slide through later." He said in a cold voice.

I knew niggas well enough to know when they had some ulterior motive. It was no

69

coincidence that my brother was over with Jaquan's crew right now.

My brother never was around any street niggas more than in passing. I stayed on his ass about the shit. So for him to all of the sudden be around Jaquan after the shit last night told me they were planning a get back at me somehow.

I nccdcd to play the shit off though. The less I acted like I felt some shit was up or suspected anything the more likely I could get him out of the situation he was in. Whatever they may have been planning for him, I prayed I could use the feelings Jaquan had for me to fix this shit.

"Okay daddy. Just hurry up. As soon as you drop him off, we can leave and go back to your spot. Like I said, I know I got some making up to do." I said not letting any of the real feelings I felt come through in my voice.

"Bet". He said before ending the call.

I almost threw my damn phone across the room when the call ended. My body was shaking and I swear I was ready to kill that nigga.

He really didn't know who he was fucking with. But there was nothing I wouldn't do for my damn brother. My hands were tied on this one, for now.

Jaquan was a real fucking bitch to play pussy last night when confronted then come at me like he was doing.

I calmed myself down enough to start thinking clearer. Even if I killed the nigga, his team would come after me.

I could never let him live and keep going on with him possibly using Terrell as a pawn later on if some other shit happened. It would be like I was in his complete control with him knowing my weakness.

There was only one thing I could do and that was to agree to moving back home to New Orleans and starting over. I didn't have time to feel sorry for losing the little bit of independence I had gained.

This shit was bigger than my feelings. Houston was now unsafe for my brother, so we needed to move. I always tried to be practical about shit.

I went ahead and called Saint's ass. He would be happy as fuck that I agreed so quickly. But I was definitely gonna let his ass know what the fuck he cost me. This was on his ass.

He came into my life when shit was fine. It may not have been perfect, but it was something.

Now I was about to be on the damn run. I would be on the run from these niggas in

Houston, because after I got Terrell back I was still gonna handle Jaquan's ass.

Him putting my brother's life in danger was enough for me to off him. There was a time when niggas and bitches fucked me over in so many ways. I had been used and abused, tortured and raped, but coming up out of all that made me what I was now. I was cold as hell.

So Jaquan was gonna die tonight. I tried getting ahold of Saint a few more times, but his ass wasn't answering. I went ahead and sent him a message.

I figured once he saw that shit, he would be headed back this way. If not, then I would just pop up on his ass back home.

After placing the call I began to prepare for playing my role. Jaquan could be here any minute. It may be in fifteen minutes or a few hours. But I was gonna be ready for his ass. He was gonna wish he never fucked with my family.

Saint

After I was on the highway headed back out Nya's way, I put in a call to Buck. Since we basically came up together Nya was like a sister to his ass too. He knew exactly who the fuck it was when I grabbed her off stage last night.

He really hadn't said shit about last night except just asking if shit was straight this morning when we were on our way back.

I didn't go into detail, but I did tell him her and Terrell were gonna be back home real soon. The nigga didn't respond other than offering a little chuckle like he thought some shit was funny.

"Yo, I'm headed back out to get Nya right now. She got a problem that needs to be handled." I said letting him know the situation in case some shit went down.

"I'm ready when you are nigga. You already know." He said back.

"Nah, I'm good on this one. But I'll get up with you when I'm on the way back."

"Word. Keep me posted." Buck responded before we both ended the call.

I was gonna be in and out before some real shit went down out there. That nigga trying some shit didn't surprise me. I wounded the weak ass niggas pride. But shit, it wasn't my fault he was bitch made. That couldn't have been me, letting some nigga punk my ass like that. Yeah the boy was a fucking bitch.

Niggas like him did hoe shit when it came to retaliation. They didn't have a code to keep shit in the streets where it belonged. I bet after I came through again he would be wishing he took the mothafuckin' loss like a G.

I was tired of driving but my adrenalin kept me going. On the way, crazy ass Martina called and texted me a few times.

I was gonna have to block her damn number and just come clean with her pops. It was time I let shit play out the way it was gonna, one way or the other. I couldn't stand letting a bitch have one up on me.

Nya hadn't answered any of my calls or texts that I sent her way. It seemed like she was on some other shit. It almost had me reconsidering whether all the trouble was worth it. Then I thought about what she really meant to me.

Nya was family and was one of the only people who I gave a fuck about in this world. So I would go to war behind her every fucking time it was needed.

As I turned on the street I spotted Nya right away. Her body stood out from a mile away. She was caked up with that bitch ass nigga from last night leaned all up against the nigga's ride.

She was laying it on thick and if I didn't know better I would have thought they were a happy ass couple out here.

Seeing her on him acting like a hoe ready to fuck, caught me off guard for a second I couldn't even lie.

I never witnessed Nya being intimate with a nigga. The closest I had been to seeing that shit was when she approached me. But this right here had my mothafuckin' trigger finger itching.

She was dressed in a short ass dress that clung to every damn curve she had. The nigga had his hands cuffing her ass and when he started to move them mothafuckas up under her skirt I lost all control.

I jumped out of my ride which was parked across the street and ran over to where the two of them were posted. Nya spotted me first since she was facing my direction. I gave a nod, and just like I wanted she backed up off of him a few feet.

That caught his attention, but not enough for a real ass nigga like me. I would have never been out here slipping over a bitch like he was. He didn't have the sense to even be ready with his piece, by the time I was within striking distance.

When he finally heard me approach it was too late. He turned his head slightly and that's when I pistol whipped his bitch ass right on his fucking temple.

The hit caused him to lose balance and stagger. Just before he fell, Nya came in and caught his weight on the side that was collapsing, using her body to keep him upright. It was lights out for the nigga after that blow.

I went and took up Nya's place to hold the brunt of the weight. I led him over to the apartment door. Nya was already opening up it up with her keys. We did all this shit as fast as possible without saying shit. It was like we knew what the other was thinking and planning without having to speak on it.

I wouldn't usually be doing all this shit out in the open especially out of town. It was still clear as day out and too many witnesses that could end up be a fucking headache later.

But seeing Nya in the nigga's face acting how she was, set me the fuck off. She should never have to be out here like that no matter what the fuck the situation.

After we got the nigga inside I sat his ass down on the only piece of furniture in sight. The apartment was small as hell and didn't have shit in it. But it was clean. Nya was a neat freak and always used to talk shit to me and Jolie.

She rubbed off on my sister so much that her ass started in on the same shit. So I wasn't surprised that even though her apartment wasn't much it was clean as hell.

"So what now?" Nya asked taking me out of my thoughts.

I looked over in her direction and let my eyes wander up and down her body for a second before I regained my train of thought. Her body was too damn much for the little ass dress she was wearing. Seeing that shit up close and personal last night didn't do shit to help the attraction I had for her.

I still wasn't trying to fuck with her like that. I couldn't even front though, I was glad as fuck that this nigga she obviously had been fucking with wasn't gonna be in the picture anymore.

"Where's Terrell?" I asked not really answering her question. I already made up my mind that this nigga was gonna die. Then we were gonna get the fuck outa Houston and let shit cool off.

I wasn't gonna come back out this way until after I sat down with my connect and came to terms about Martina and expanding out here. So it should give me a few days to let the dust settle.

"He's in the back, in his room. Jaquan dropped him off. I was gonna handle his ass once we got back to his spot." She said with way too much damn confidence for me.

"Really, Nya. You gonna handle a nigga that's twice ya size shawty?!, Nah, I'm gonna handle this nigga for you. And then ya'll getting the fuck outa this place for good, ya heard." I responded back letting my voice show that I meant fucking business. I didn't wanna hear shit else about it.

Nya always had them hands but that was completely different than taking a nigga's life. I didn't know much about the last ten years of her life, but she wasn't a killer, that was for damn sure.

I could respect the fact that she wanted to handle shit though. At least that told me she was on her shit and not just a dumb hoe trying to use her pussy to get out of shit. All the shit she was doing outside was an act and hearing her confirm that made me relieved.

Me pulling up when I did was perfect fucking timing. A few minutes later and she probably would've been on the way to the bitch nigga's house. The thought had me ready to kill the nigga right now.

"Get Terrell and go out to my ride." I said.

Nya didn't fucking move. Instead she walked over to where that pussy nigga was knocked out on the couch. He was still out of it, in a sitting position with his head leaned forward limp. His chin was touching his chest since he was still unconscious.

Nya grabbed ahold of his chin and lifted his head up. Then she reached up with her other hand and pulled a razor from her hair that was tied up in a bun on top of her head.

It was like watching a fucking movie the way Nya ran the blade across the nigga's throat without a second thought. Even though he was out of it, the blood seeped out and he began to gurgle from the breath his brain wasn't getting.

After a minute or two all movement stopped and Nya wiped the blade on the couch back, next to his dead body.

Then she put the razor right back in her hair like the shit she did was nothing to her. When she was finished she turned around and started walking back towards me.

She stopped right in front of me and leaned in to whisper in my ear, while she reached out and grabbed my dick through my pants.

"I knew that shit turned you on." She said in a completely different voice than I had ever heard her use before.

Hell yeah she was right, my dick was hard as fuck. But it wasn't just because the shit she just did and what I witnessed. I never could control the mothafucka around Nya. She was the only female ever that kept my dick hard and my head fucked up.

I wanted to bend her ass over and lay the dick on her right here. But I wasn't about to take it there with her.

Her bossing up and the way she left that nigga leaking like she just did only made me want her more. I stood in the same place almost paralyzed from wanting to break my rules when it came to her.

Thankfully, I got myself back together by the time she came out from the back with her little brother.

Her ass had put on a track suit, which was a good thing because sitting next to her the whole ride back was gonna be a challenge as it was.

I never held back when it came to touching, and handling a woman the way I wanted when I wanted. This shit with Nya was fucking with me bad.

After I put both their bags in the trunk, I got in the car. Nya and Terrell were already in my ride waiting to head to New Orleans.

Right before we left I set a fire to the apartment with a piece of paper that I left on the isle of the stove. I made sure the flames overtook the apartment before we finally pulled off.

I wanted to erase as much of Nya's DNA as possible away from Jaquan's body when the police found the shit. The charred remains wouldn't lead to shit.

I hoped the mothafuckas thought some shit happened to Nya, or at least I hoped she wouldn't feel no heat behind the murder. There was never a way to be a hundred percent sure. But it was too late to be worried about that shit.

The nigga signed his death warrant when he came after my fucking family. I couldn't even take credit for this one though. It was all Nya. She showed the fuck out and left me wondering how she came to be so deadly.

Some shit had definitely changed to cause her to go hard like that. I witnessed a whole other side to shawty. She was just as cold as me now.

Within a few minutes we were on the highway, already on our way back home. New Orleans was just as much Nya and Terrell's home as it was mine. It was the place all three of us fucking belonged.

Nya's whole damn life was going to change. When she left all those years ago, I was just starting to get money and make moves in the streets. But not anything worth bragging about. Not that I was a bragging ass nigga.

But now, I ran shit and my money was longer than she could imagine. Yeah shawty was in for a big fucking surprise.

Nya

I knew that Saint was turned on by me. I wasn't surprised in the least when I grabbed his dick and verified what I already knew. What surprised the hell out of me was how big he was. I mean that shit was the biggest I ever felt and I didn't even get a look at it.

I bet he thought I was a typical hoe out here from how he saw me at the strip club and now out all up on Jaquan the way I was. But that was the furthest thing from reality.

In truth, I had only been intimate with a few men willingly in my life. I never sold pussy or shit like that. When it came to sex, I didn't even enjoy it that much.

I knew it had to do with how my aunt had done me when she first brought us out to Houston with her.

The day after we arrived, and the day after me and my little brother buried our parents I was confronted with the harsh reality of the life that I had been thrown into.

It became apparent from that day on, that my aunt was pure evil and had no intention of caring for me or Terrell the way she pretended she was going to, to my father's family. It turned out she was just a jealous envious bitch who couldn't stand my mother. I picked up on that shit from the jump.

The first man I had sex with, was a middle aged random nigga that paid my aunt for some young pussy. I tried to fight him off the best I could when he came into the tiny room my aunt designated for me on that night, but no matter how many punches I threw or kicks I landed he was fucking relentless.

Eventually, he got tired of trying to hold me down against my will and instead closed fist punched me in the eye knocking me unconscious.

When I work up naked with blood between my legs, I knew exactly what had happened. I was fifteen, a child, being molested by a man sent in by the woman who was charged with my care. My own fucking family at that.

Looking out the window on the way back to New Orleans, I couldn't help being caught up in my own thoughts, reliving some of my past.

I knew that the questions would come, if not now and not from Saint, then they would be coming from Jolie. I was excited as hell to reunite with my bestie, but a part of me was scared to death.

No matter what shit I went through I still felt like I betrayed her and our friendship by the way shit went down. I just hoped she could get past that shit. Because to me she was always my one and only sister.

That was another reason why me and Saint had a really complicated ass relationship. I knew he looked at me like a little sister and he had always been a big brother in my life coming up. There were so many times when he looked out for me that I couldn't even fucking count.

But from the age of about ten until I left, I began looking at him in a different way too. He gave me these looks that sent chills down my spine and when my body began to change I really thought he had the same type of feelings for me.

He still confused the fuck out of me. It was like the attraction and desire between us was undeniable, but that stupid nigga always denied the shit. That left me feeling not good enough. Like I wasn't what he wanted or the type of woman who was enough for him.

Even now, sitting next to him caused my body to respond without him doing a fucking thing. It was like my pussy knew when he was near. I never experienced no shit like this other than when I was around his ass.

Now that I felt what he was working with my thoughts kept going back to what it would feel like to have him inside me.

I must have closed my eyes and dozed off, because when I opened them back up it was to Saint gently shaking me and speaking softly, just above a whisper.

The car was stopped and he was leaned over enough that I felt his breath on my cheek. When my eyes opened, I came face to face with the one nigga who was a blessing and a damn curse at the same time in my life.

He gave me one of those corny ass smiles that he always did back when we were kids and all I could do was smile right back at his ass, like a goofy kid myself.

Saint looked like money, smelled like money and everything about him screamed "boss." When we were kids he and Jolie barely had enough money to buy clothes or food. That was why he started hustling.

I remember clear as day the money he first brought in off the block. He gave me and Jolie each a hundred dollars and kept like twenty five dollars for himself apart from his re-up money. I never understood why he gave me any of what he earned.

I lived a couple streets over from where Jolie and Saint stayed, but there was a big difference in our situations. Both my parents worked at regular ass jobs and made okay money. We never went without like Saint and Jolie did.

So when he laid the cash in my hand, I tried to refuse and give it right the fuck back. I didn't need shit and wasn't trying to take away from the ends he was making for his own family. But this nigga immediately shut that shit down. I even remembered the conversation like it was yesterday.

"Why you give me this? Here... I'm not taking your money Saint." I said as soon as he placed the bills in my hand. It looked like a whole lot more than the hundred that he told me it was. It was stacks of ones and tens mostly.

"Nah, that's you. You know I got you shawty." He said back to my ass with a serious ass look before turning around like the conversation was over.

"Saint!" I called out as he walked away. I was determined to not take his money when I knew how hard he worked and how much he and Jolie needed every little bit.

He looked back over his shoulder and gave me an ice cold stare that shut me the hell up. I was stuck and didn't say nothing else about the money.

I knew from his look that there would be no convincing him, to not give me money.

Now shit had switched up. He was definitely a boss, while I was barely surviving.

I didn't wish nothing but the best for him. He deserved every fucking thing he got. Saint really was the best kind of man in my eyes.

He held shit down and handled his responsibilities.

There wasn't shit he wouldn't do for the people he loved. There was another side to him too. The heartless gangsta that killed in the blink of an eye. But that side of him was never directed at me.

Not even a small part of me felt salty about his come up despite my struggle. It was just the way shit played out. I wasn't bitter about my situation.

I used to feel sorry for myself, but the day when Terrell came in and almost caught a nigga raping me, something in me snapped. That was the day I decided not to be a damn victim anymore.

It took me 6 months to get my head on right when we moved to Houston and once I made that decision, we moved the hell out of my aunt's house and I began taking care of the both of us on my own.

I let my eyes roam over Saint's face for a good minute and he kept his gaze right back on me. He sat back in his seat, but still turned his head enough to keep his eyes locked with mine. Almost like he was daring me to speak and say some shit he wasn't' gonna like.

But all that was on my mind was how sexy this nigga was. I looked at his juicy lips and then boldly looked up and down his body like his ass did me all the time when he thought I wasn't looking. I admired how his body filled out. He was full of solid muscle, but not too overbearing. His light skin and dimples added to his appeal.

He had a nice light caramel complexion like a lotta niggas from New Orleans that were mixed with a whole bunch of shit.

Most people thought Saint was mean as hell because of how he carried himself. He was a shooter from an early age, so I knew why he got that reputation.

He was always soft when it came to me and his sister. I couldn't lie though, him being a real ass gangsta drew me to him even more. I liked a nigga that was real and had good character. But I needed a man that had that edge to him too. I would never be with a lame ass dude, not for real anyway.

The car was filled with an awkward silence, but I could tell Saint still had something on his mind, so I waited for him to tell me what it was. In the meantime, I would just enjoy looking at his sexy ass.

As we sat in a comfortable but tension filled silence, Saint lit up a blunt and then told me the shit that I was waiting on. I didn't know if I should be happy or mad as fuck about the shit.

"You know I got love for you Nya, but that shit back there aint fittin' happen shawty. I'm gonna take care of you and lil bruh. Ya'll gon' stay with Jolie for now. In the meantime get ya'self together and focus on getting your life together. No more bullshit jobs or bitch ass niggas." He said trying to tell me what the hell to do like usual.

I swear the only shit that had changed about Saint over the years was his status and that he got even better looking. But his dominance was exactly the same as I remembered. When he said some shit, he said it in a way that left no room for a conversation or disagreement to happen.

I folded my arms over my chest and began shaking my right leg. That was a habit I had that came out whenever I was trying not to lose my cool and flip out.

It was one thing for Saint to be trying to look out for me and Terrell. But all that other shit he was coming at me with I wasn't trying to hear. The shit that pissed me off the most, was the nerve of him to once again have me feeling like I wasn't good enough for him and that he didn't want me.

On top of that he added in the part about me not fucking with any niggas. Saint didn't want me, but he didn't want me with anyone else. What kind of bullshit was that?

I didn't reply at all. He took a few more pulls of the blunt and then went to put the shit out by rolling down his window. I hurried up and reached across his body and took it right out of his hand before he had the chance to throw it out.

"Just like old times" He chuckled.

"What's that suppose to mean?" I asked with a bad ass attitude in defense.

"Damn Nya, chill the fuck out with all that attitude. I ain't the one. Can't even joke with your sensitive ass anymore, why you tripping?"

It felt like home already and I took a few deep pulls smoking a little of the blunt. The effects of the weed started to calm me down and I was almost able to forget the dumb shit Saint said to me that had me heated.

Saint spoke up again, I guess figuring I wasn't gonna say shit back to his ass. Which was definitely better for him than if I did let him know what was on my mind.

""I'm a drop you off over sis house now, she's waiting for ya'll. Tomorrow I'll come by and get shit settled." He said again as a statement. Not asking me shit or seeing if I had an opinion one way or the other.

I rolled my window down like he had done a few minutes before and threw the last little bit of the blunt out. It was dark outside and we were the only car parked over on this side of the building. I recognized the spot as the corner store from my old neighborhood. Ready or not, I was home.

A few minutes later Saint pulled up into a small driveway behind a nice ass Benz. The house was one I had never seen before. It looked like it was newly built. I figured this was Jolie's house. It was just down the road from my childhood home and two streets over from where we spent all our time as kids.

After Hurricane Katrina there was a bunch of demolished houses and empty lots in our neighborhood. Shit, it was like that in all the damn neighborhoods down here. Most of the folk around here didn't have the funds to rebuild, so they moved away.

We stayed in a few of the houses that weren't overrun with mold and actually held up during the storm. My parents rented the place I grew up in. Even Saint's and Jolie's grandfather didn't own his shit. The hurricane wiped out entire communities and made it harder for all the original black neighborhoods to survive.

I had a feeling that Jolie owned this place. That in itself was a big ass accomplishment for any one of us to have. I couldn't wait to see my girl and catch up. I was excited to hear all about her life and how shit was going for her. Whether she had a bomb ass job or what. I'm sure Saint had something to do wither how well she was doing too.

Once the car was in park, I didn't even turn to look over at Saint or ask any questions before I hopped my ass out of the car. I opened the back door to where Terrell was laid out in the backseat. I playfully woke him up by kissing on his cheeks. He hated when I babied him. Even though he was a teenager, Terrell was still like a damn little ass child to me. Shit, I raised his ass.

He wiped away the kisses and then got up out the car headed up to the front of the house. I guess Saint wasn't feeling the fact that I was ignoring his ass. He knew me and how stubborn I was, so he should have expected that shit.

I was intentionally giving his ass the cold shoulder. Fuck Saint. That was my go-to thought all the time when he said or did some shit that I didn't like. Ain't shit changed about that either.

Terrel was almost as excited to see Jolie as I was. We talked about our memories to avoid forgetting and to remember the good times as something to motivate us. I especially replayed memories to him over the years to keep both our spirits up when shit was tough. Even though he was only 7 when we moved to Houston he still had enough memories of Jolie to be excited to see her ass.

Just before I made it to the bottom step, following Terrell, Saint grabbed my elbow from behind. I turned my head around but not my body. I wasn't gonna let this nigga rain on my damn parade any more tonight.

Saying shit that I considered disrespectful and like I didn't have any damn sense. This nigga really acted like I was just some hoe out here with bad judgment.

Getting with a man was the last thing on my mind. But best believe if I wanted to do some shit I would. Saint wouldn't stop shit over this way.

"Get rid of that attitude shawty. I'm here for you now. You aint gotta be outa pocket or character. Ya dig."

"Good looking I guess. I get what you saying, but you should know me better than that! But it's all good." I said with a shrug and a fake ass smile.

I was actually grateful that shit happened the way it did. With the complications and all, Saint running in to me last night before I completely lost all my pride stripping in that club. Also, for coming to get me when Jaquan pulled that pussy shit.

But he needed to do better with how he was treating me and coming at me. I wasn't a bitch to tolerate disrespect even from his ass. I wasn't mad, but he better recognize I was still the same Nya in a lot of ways and he should do better by me.

How could I be mad at him though. He thought the same shit that most other mothafuckas thought about me. I would give him a pass this one time on that shit and try not to care what the fuck Saint thought anymore.

I couldn't let his ass hurt my feelings. I needed to be stronger than what I was feeling.

I turned back around and walked up the steps to meet up with my best friend. Terrel knocked on the door a few times, and Jolie threw that shit back yelling and screaming.

She gave Terrell a quick hug before releasing him and running the two steps down to meet me before I got to the damn door. I swear this bitch was the most. But I loved her.

"Oh my Gawd!!!!! My sister came back to me. Yasssssss." She pulled me into the house with her holding onto my hand.

Terrell already made his way in and was sitting on the couch like he was really at home.

I shook my head at him, letting out a laugh before sitting down to get comfortable myself. It had been a long ass 24 hours. There wasn't even time for a tour of her house on nothing.

I prepared myself for the questions, because as soon as my best friend sat down I knew they were gonna come. I guess it was time to shed some light onto my life and where the fuck I had been for the last ten years.

Saint

What I felt for Nya was nothing but love. Having lil' baby ride with me all the way back home made me feel at peace the most a nigga like me could. That shit may not make sense, but Nya was always mine even though she wasn't my girl.

I loved the shit out of her. I loved her as part of my family and more than that. I always went back and forth thinking about what my life could be like with her in it as my woman. Even with distance and time I still thought about her ass from time to time. From how she was doing and all that random shit that a nigga who really cared about a bitch and had deep feelings for did.

Did I love Nya? That shit was a done fucking deal a long ass time ago for me. But was I gonna be her nigga and really be with her in that way? I didn't think I would ever take it there with her.

To me she was worth more than all the shit I had to offer. I had the bread to take care of her beyond her wildest dreams, but I wasn't built for that love shit. She deserved the fucking best and I didn't think I was the best for her.

I came with too much shit. Not only the street shit and all the risk involved, but I was a cold hearted nigga when it came down to it.

I made a pledge to myself when our parents left that I would never wife a bitch. All the way from when I was a little ass kid I decided I didn't want nothing to do with being weak, and that included letting a bitch fuck me over. I wasn't ever gonna be out of pocket or put my heart out there for a woman to cause me pain. No bitch would be my downfall.

I saw that love and relationship shit as a deathtrap. That's how shit worked out for my parents. Both of them were always chasing a nigga or bitch instead of being damn parents to their kids. Then it turned into them chasing the high. Fuck that shit.

Even now that I was grown I still saw the shit for what it was. Whenever I looked around me it was always some bitch fucking over her nigga and him losing his mind behind the shit. Or it was the other way around, and the nigga couldn't do right by his old lady causing nothing but pain in her life.

All that shit just made mothafuckas weak. I didn't have time for that shit. So I was good keeping things the way they were between me and Nya.

Riding with her all the way back, my eyes kept finding their way back over to look at her body and her sexy exposed thighs. They looked soft as hell and her dark skin glowed from the interior lights. Nya was the worst kind of temptation for me.

Now that I saw what was under those clothes yesterday and watched the way she bossed up and killed that fuck nigga it only made me want her more. That shit might've seemed crazy as hell, but I wasn't a typical nigga. A weak bitch was a turn off. Then Nya got all bold and shit grabbing my dick. This bitch was the damn truth.

I needed to keep my distance from shawty from here on out, otherwise I knew it would only be a matter of time before shit went too far. There was no way around it. We were both way too grown now and it would only be a matter of time before I went back and broke my own rules to the shit.

After tomorrow, when I took her to get all the shit she needed and set her up, I would just check on her through Jolie for a while.

Otherwise there was no telling what I would do and the last thing I wanted to do was hurt Nya. That was even more important than any other reason I had for not fucking with her.

Earlier I dipped out on Martina's crazy ass right after we finished fucking. Now that I was back in town, I needed to head home and make some shit shake on the business tip. My house was near Jolie's since we both still lived in the hood. But my place was more on the outskirts a few streets over where there was more land.

I had a custom built house that was nice as hell. I still had the contractor's that built my shit keep it modest on the outside. But on the inside, my house was set the fuck up.

Nobody on my team except Buck even came inside the bitch. Too many niggas had that envious side to them and would do anything to find a way to take all the shit I worked hard for.

I kept a low profile for the most part just like most of the niggas on my team. I had a reputation of being a shooter, a nigga that would go to blows when necessary and a boss.

To them, I was just a nigga that ran shit and had some money. These niggas didn't have a clue how much bread I was really bringing in or the high status I was trying to build up to in the organized crime world. That was how I was gonna keep it too. The last thing I wanted was a big fucking target on my back in my own hood.

I was a gangsta and liked to be in the streets daily, I wasn't trying to change up none of that shit.

So far the arrangement I had with the other bosses around the city, kept shit sweet. But I knew that could change up at any minute. Any nigga that got too comfortable in this lifestyle was asking to be taken out. So needless to say, I never was comfortable. You couldn't afford to be. I didn't trust any mothafuckas besides Buck and my sister.

Now that Nya was back, even she was gonna have to earn my trust back. I still loved the girl, but she had been gone for a long ass time. People can change. I wanted to think the best of her, but the fact was the old Nya wouldn't have been up on stage stripping disrespecting herself and the old Nya wouldn't have taken a life without fucking blinking.

There definitely was some shit that she went through that left a mark on her life. I was fine seeing her boss up and be a strong ass woman holding her own. But I hoped that she was still the same down ass bitch she used to be too. The type that held shit down through thick and thin, that I had known before.

Nya seemed so fucking different, but not at all at the same time. Shit was confusing as fuck. Now the way she looked only got fucking better, her body filled out even more. She was hands down the finest bitch around.

I pulled into my drive and got out of my whip. I closed the door and then walked into my house. I finally could kick back and relax for a minute. Once inside my master bedroom, I changed out of my clothes. Then I went back downstairs to chill out while I handled the business shit that had been heavy on my mind. I poured myself a glass of cognac and got comfortable in my favorite chair in the living room.

I went ahead and sent my plug a message asking for a meeting one on one. It took him about thirty minutes to get back to me. He never hit me right back and I knew he did that shit to show me he was the boss.

There was certain things niggas with power did to try and keep those under him; under him.

He replied back agreeing to meet up on Monday morning. That meant I had one day to get shit settled and decide how I was gonna put everything out there for him.

I wanted to continue working with Pedro if possible. But the main shit I needed to figure out was how to keep his whole damn cartel from coming after me and my team.

My team was big here in New Orleans, but compared to a fucking cartel we weren't shit. I may not have liked the shit, but it was facts. There was no way we could compete with them in a war. We would all be dead before the shit even started.

I wasn't a bitch about a damn thing, but there was no way I was willing to go to war behind Martina or no pussy for that matter. If it was some shit to do with money, respect or a move I was making then so be it. But this shit wasn't worth the trouble as it was.

I hit Buck up and told him to round up our lieutenants for a team meeting tomorrow at our main trap. Then I went into my office to look over all my legal business shit. I had investments in stocks and bonds, a strip club and a local restaurant I opened a year ago. I wasn't hands on with most of the shit I dealt in and kept most of my attention on my illegal shit.

But when my money was involved I still kept oversight. Other than that, I hired the best mothafuckas to help make me more money. Plus the goal was to keep the feds off my back as long as possible. There was only so much dough a nigga could bring in without catching attention from 5-O.

I knew as long as I was in this lifestyle I would most likely end up going back to the penitentiary sooner or later. This life usually led two places. It was rare for a nigga to actually make it out on top. That shit only happened with the niggas pulling strings or some straight syndicate shit. Not niggas like me that built shit from the ground up and came from nothing.

More than likely I was gonna die or end up locked up for the shit I was into. Maybe I would be able to beat the odds and be smart enough to make the right moves to stay on top, but that wasn't how shit usually went.

One thing about me was I was realistic about shit. Too many niggas were dumb and cocky. They tried to do too much not thinking they could be touched. I wasn't one of them. I stayed ready for whatever and if the time came, I was ready to die, or ready to take my time with my head held high and my lips sealed.

I finally finished going over all the paperwork and put it away for the night. I only went over the books and portfolio shit on my laptop once a week. It was something I hated to do, but always stayed on top of.

I didn't trust the accountants and people I hired enough not to fuck me over. So I let one of them run the books and then had another to check their work. None of the people that worked for me knew each other. I was paranoid as fuck.

I went ahead and poured another glass of liquor. My thoughts went back to Nya. I wondered how much information Jolie was getting out of her. My sister and Nya were close as fuck, and if any person could get some details about how shawty was living these past ten years it was her.

Hopefully Nya was actually opening up and telling Jolie what was up. I needed to get in her ear about the shit too. I knew there was more to what Nya was saying and if there was some shit to handle for her than that's what the fuck I was gonna do.

In the meantime she better take me serious with what the fuck I told her ass. She needed to get herself straight and that was all her ass had time for. I would stand by my words and she should know that shit.

If she tried pulling some slick shit and a nigga came in the picture, he would be out of it before she even knew what the fuck happened. I had so many bodies under my belt another one didn't mean shit to me.

But Nya knew when I said shit I meant it, so I wasn't too worried about her trying me.

She did catch me off guard with how bold she was when she came up and grabbed my dick. That attraction and shit used to be some juvie type shit, but now she was a full grown woman.

I saw the look of surprise on her face when she realized what the fuck I was working with. Lil baby should know everything about me was gonna be on point. She regained her composure quick as hell, but I bet her pussy was a different story.

Staying away and remaining only friends was gonna be hard, but I had done it in the past. I just needed to get back some of my regular hoes in rotation to keep myself from slipping up.

I finished my drink and tried to get everything settled for the next day. In the morning I was gonna scoop Nya up and take care of her first. Then I planned to get up with my crew and let them in on some of the new plans. Shit was on a need to know basis only.

At best my plug, Pedro, wouldn't let personal shit get in the way of all the money I was making his ass. But most mothafucka's weren't gonna let shit like this slide.

I was fucking his daughter after all and no father wants to hear that shit. I had to approach the situation in a way that didn't make me seem disrespectful.

I needed to be realistic and make plans for the other possibility also. Pedro would most likely become my enemy tomorrow and there wasn't a doubt in my mind what that meant. The minute I became his enemy he was gonna try and take me and my crew out.

I was determined to make shit work out in my favor. So I didn't think twice about putting my plan B in motion ahead of time. I went ahead and dialed the only nigga I knew who might be able to help me out.

"Yo, I got a problem." I said into the phone to the unfamiliar voice. I should have been more comfortable talking to the nigga. But that shit didn't matter right now. I needed to look out for my operation and my team. I would put all that personal shit to the side for the time being.

Nya

After spending the first two hours catching up with Jolie it was now getting late as hell. So far she hadn't pressed me on anything to get details about where the hell I'd been or what I'd been up to. I gave vague answers and kept shit short and to the point.

I was grateful that she didn't push me to tell her everything. I didn't wanna relive old wounds or have a damn pity party. I was past the shit or at least I trying to be.

I did let her know that life had been tough for me and Terrell and that I ended up dropping out of school to get a job and take care of him.

I told her enough about my aunt Renae for her to know that she wasn't shit and didn't have good intentions with us from the beginning. She was jealous and hated my mother. So I had to step up and be the caregiver for my brother.

Terrel went ahead and got comfortable settling in as soon as Jolie showed him the room he was staying in. She had shit set up like she was ready for us the whole damn time. I don't know how she did it, but she already had a big ass flat screen and playstation in his room. It was decked out with all the shit a typical teenage boy would like. Even with a damn laptop.

She must have went out and copped all the shit after talking to me for that brief conversation when Saint called her. Even she knew his ass was gonna be bringing my ass back.

I almost cried when I saw how much shit she had already done for us, but the wall I had built up over the years wouldn't let me. I loved Jolie and she truly was my damn sister, but a part of me was still having a hard time letting her all the way back in.

She never did anything for me to have my guard up. It was just that for so long I had to keep the real me protected and not let a mothafucka see a weakness.

I was hestitant, but I hoped with time I could get back to being the more open and unsuspecting girl I once was. I didn't want to be cold and distant.

We had been sipping on some mascoto and I could honestly say I was enjoying having my best friend back in my life already. We got caught up recalling old childhood memories and of course all of them included her hard headed ass brother.

Thinking about Saint caused my body to respond just like it did when I sat next to his ass the whole way back from Texas.

Shaking the thoughts of him away, I tried to pay attention to the last question Jolie asked me because the time had finally come to give her at least a little bit of insight.

"I get you was out there on your own girl. But why didn't you call a bitch? I mean you know me and Saint was here for you. I love you no matter what, but damn it was like you didn't want shit else to do with us. You still my girl, my sister, but shit. What the fuck was up with that?" Jolie asked and I could hear the hurt in her voice.

I understood what she was asking and this was exactly how I knew she was gonna feel. She felt like I turned my back on her. I mean what kind of best friend doesn't even attempt to make a damn phone call, not even one time.

What could I say in my defense? So instead of telling her all the details about why I felt like I couldn't, I gave an honest but sheltered answer.

"Jolie you gotta know I love you girl. You ARE my damn sister. But the shit that happened to me, to us..." I corrected referring to me and Terrel, "Just know that it was bad enough that I COULDN"T call. Believe me... I would have." I said through tears by the time I finished.

This was the shit I didn't even like to think about anymore. I was a broken woman and Jolie was getting to see me for what I was now.

Even though I seemed good, I wasn't. Just mentioning that time period in my life was still painful as hell and brought back old feelings like the shit just happened yesterday.

There was no way to erase the pain that's caused by being violated by a man, especially when I was still a child. Just like there was no way to erase the day in and day out struggle that I endured trying to take care of Terrell at sixteen with nothing to my damn name.

Jolie came over to where I was sitting on the couch and wrapped me up in her arms. We sat there hugging for a few minutes. It felt good as hell to have her accept me despite how I turned my back on her.

"Alright, we good Nya. We good." She repeated and thankfully didn't ask any more questions trying to get more out of me.

After her last question and my answer our conversation ended and we both got up ready for bed. We cleaned up the wine and snacks that were scattered on the living room table.

Jolie had tomorrow off before having to go back to work on Monday. So she was gonna come with me and Saint. She reassured me that we would be spending Saint's money like "usual" and none of her own.

Jolie was so over the top and outgoing with shit. When she emphasized that it was

Saint's money I couldn't do nothing but laugh.

"Bitch you know I'm running up a check in there. Okay! I know he already got you fucked up with his stupid ass too. I saw that exchange ya'll had." She continued trying to cheer me up, but making me think about her brother in the process.

"He just don't know how to talk to me, and I had to make him remember." I confirmed.

"But you know he loves him some NYASIA!!! Don't take it personal, he must've got dropped on his head as a baby. That's why that shit so damn big and he say dumb shit all the time." She answered jokingly.

"Mmmmhhhhm. Must be the reason." I added.

It was all love though. Jolie always talked shit when it came to Saint. But let a bitch say some shit or do something she didn't like concerning him and it was all over for the hoe.

I was in on the shit too back in the day. We handled bitches older than us two at a time. That was my girl and she was the shit.

Jolie's house was three bedrooms, so I had my own room to sleep in. It looked like a typical guest room.

Right before we headed into our rooms Jolie took the time to reassure me again that she was happy as hell to have me back where I belonged according to her. I settled into my surroundings, more comfortable than I had been in a long ass time.

I decided to take a nice hot shower to wash away any remnants of my old life. Including the body that I just had added to the other's I had under my belt. I wasn't an all-out killer or nothing, but there were a few niggas that I took care of out of necessity, Jaquan included.

There was a time when I let men walk all over me, but I learned to handle my own right after I left my aunt's house for good.

I ended up using all of the hot water before I finally stepped out of the shower. It felt so damn good to let the hot water run over my body and think about me and Terrell's future.

I was starting to have some hope again. Before running into Saint, I had really gotten to a point that I barely recognized myself anymore.

There was a time in my life where I would have never considered showing my body for dollar bills. I wanted to get back to who I was before, or at least who I could be.

I stood in front of the mirror and used some of the shea butter moisturizer and spread it all over my ebony skin. As I rubbed the lotion over my thick thighs and fat ass I thought back to the looks that Saint continued to give me when he thought I wasn't looking. Yeah that nigga wanted me, just like I had always wanted him.

Shit his dick was proof of the attraction he felt. Then his ass hit me with that speech about not fucking around and for me not to see another nigga in the same damn sentence.

As I finished up with the lotion I moved my hand down to my pussy while I stood in the mirror admiring my reflection.

I began working two of my fingers in and out of my entrance, while rubbing my breasts with the other hand.

I had full D cups and a fat ass. Otherwise most people considered me slim thick because of my height and size everywhere else. I was petite except those two assets.

A man's touch never did shit for me before. I wasn't a hoe but had been with a few niggas willingly. All that sex shit didn't get me off the way I could get myself off.

I swear I could still smell that Saint's cologne from earlier. As my thoughts stayed on Saint, I pictured his body and even his crooked smile in my mind.

My body became even more aroused and juices coated my fingers. I worked my fingers faster, playing with my clit alternating between playing in my pussy and rubbing it. My breathing picked up. I leaned forward putting one hand on the counter to hold my balance while I brought myself to a peak recalling the way Saint's dick felt and how big it was when I held it in my hand.

Just before I was able to cum and reach my climax, my phone began to vibrate on the counter in front of me taking my mind off of Saint.

That was enough distraction to fuck up the sensations I had worked up. I looked to the side where the phone was and saw none other than Saint's name pop up on the screen.

I grumbled aloud... I swear, "THIS NIGGA!"

I gave up on trying to bring myself some sexual relief that was built up from earlier, caused by the only man who ever turned me on.

I picked the phone up quick and still out of breath with an attitude.

"What?!" I all but yelled into the phone.

"Damn shawty, kill the attitude." He said not feeling the way I came at him.

"Whatever nigga. Why you calling me now anyway? Maybe I was busy shit." I said. He had no idea how busy I really was or that I was touching myself, thinking about his ass.

"You bet not be busy. Let me find out you still hardheaded. Nah you not dumb. You was probably just thinking 'bout the fucking lumber you felt earlier." He said trying to play it off.

But the truth was his ass must have been thinking about my ass to be calling me. I wasn't naïve to the shit, and he definitely didn't need to know I had been doing more than thinking about him.

"Yeah okay. That shit wasn't nothing to me. Matter of fact, you probably thinking 'bout this pussy since you got a lil' glimpse, Since you calling me and shit." I said right back.

That instantly caused his whole tone to switch up. It was like night and day how he got all serious and sounded pissed off.

"I'll be by at 10 so be ready." Click. He didn't even say bye or give me a chance to respond.

Yeah he was mad. I guess him thinking about me stripping got him in his feelings and shit. Oh well we weren't anything more than friends anyway and never would be according to him.

So he better just get over the shit. I would never feel bad or apologize for the decisions I made to feed me and my little brother. I didn't like the shit either, but that was fucking life.

I went and put my phone on the charger and threw on the pajamas that Jolie left in the room for me. It was bad that I didn't even have a pair of clean drawers to my name.

I hated depending on anyone for shit, but with Jolie and Saint it didn't bother me like it would with any other person. They looked out for me out of love. Like a real brother and sister. So I would let them be here for me and Terrell and help us until I got settled and on my feet.

Best believe once I had shit in order, there wouldn't be no more handouts on my end.

Laying in the queen size bed knowing that me and Terrell were finally good was a huge relief. It all felt right. To be here and to be back with the two people that meant something to me outside my little brother.

I drifted off into a comfortable sleep and of course Saint's face was the last thing I thought about before sleep came.

When I rolled over and realized that it was already 9:30, I quickly jumped up out the bed. I stretched my arms and back then went into the bathroom to hurry up and get my ass ready for Saint to arrive.

He didn't really say shit else except to be ready, but I figured he was just taking me to get the things I needed.

116

After taking a quick shower I remembered I didn't have shit to put on. So I wrapped the towel around my body and walked out into the main part of Jolie's house hoping to find her and see what my best friend had that I could borrow to wear.

When I got to the end of the hall, the bathroom door across from me came open. Saint's ass stood there with a look of surprise and lust all over his face. He was caught off guard and the shit was funny as hell to me.

I smirked at his ass and just to be petty and mess with him, I opened up my towel with no shame and gave him a good look of my entire body up close and personal. Since he wanted to talk all that shit last night this was payback.

The truth was the man in front of me was the only man I had ever been truly attracted, both physically and emotionally. He turned me down back in the day.

The day my parents were laid to rest and I put my feelings out there he tried to act like he didn't look at me like I did him. That shit pissed me the fuck off because it was obvious he did have some kind of feelings for me and he just didn't want to admit it.

Now that we were both adults, I was just gonna keep fucking with him until he admitted the shit. It was a pride thing for me, not to mention it was funny as hell because

117

the nigga was just too damn stubborn for his own good.

I held the towel open long enough for his eyes to roam over my body, then closed it back covering myself back up. His eyes were glued to me just like I intended them to be. If Terrell or Jolie would have come out they wouldn't have seen shit since I did it in a way that was meant for his eyes only.

His look went from surprise and desire to cold as hell within a few moments just like how his tone changed last night on the phone.

I unintentionally backed up a few steps from the intimidating glare he was giving me. But Saint grabbed ahold of me wrapping me tight as fuck in his arms. He pulled me all the way into his body.

I was so close that I felt his hard dick pressing against my stomach. Yeah the mothafucka was hard and ready just like I knew. There was no denying the shit no matter what the fuck this man had to say.

He stood a good foot taller than me even though I was a decent height. He was just tall and big. Full of nothing but muscle. He must have been around 6'4" and here I was being completely enveloped by him.

A chill went down my spine and Saint still kept a tight ass grip on me not letting any space between us. Fast as hell, he moved one of his hands up under my towel in the front. I swear to god this nigga made me fucking cum the minute he touched my pussy. That shit didn't even make sense how much of an affect he had on me.

My body was all out shaking as he stuck his fingers in me like I had done to myself last night thinking about his ass. Now having him doing the shit for real was almost too much for me to take.

Of course there wasn't any going back on his damn word though. He was gonna try and prove his point with his stubborn ass. So just as quick as he slid them mothafuckas in, he pulled them out and licked the juices off each one in my face. I knew he was on that bullshit.

The look of desire he had before was gone. It was like he turned the shit off, and it had me rethinking whether he really did give a fuck about me or think about me in that way. He always had me second guessing myself I swear.

"Just like I thought. Cut the shit Nya. I told you I ain't fucking with you shawty. You my family and shit gonna stay that way. Stop throwing ya'self at a nigga. It ain't a good look, ya heard." He said with a seriousness.

I searched his face for one ounce of untruth in the shit he was telling me. I wanted more than anything for Saint to feel about me the way I felt about him. Yeah I was just trying to fuck around and play around, showing him some shit and opening my towel.

But on the real, I was in love with this nigga and had been since I could remember. Even throughout the years, I knew that what I felt for Saint I would probably never feel for another man in my lifetime.

But playing around or being serious, he wasn't going for it. I felt rejected and unwanted and I needed to stop putting myself out there even joking around at this point.

This man wasn't gonna ever wanna be with me. I realized in that moment that it was time to put my foolishness in chasing him out the window. I would take this loss and keep shit on the straight and narrow between us from here on out. Just like he wanted.

At the end of the day he was still my friend and like family to me, so I would have to get over the shit. I couldn't even feel some way about him shutting me down because he never did shit to lead me on or disrespect me. I looked up into his eyes after listening to his statement and smiled at him.

"Okay, you win Saint. I'll stop messing with you. We good. I won't surprise you no more." I said.

You damn right I played the shit off, like hearing him say he didn't want me didn't hurt. He smiled back and then walked right on past me, leaving me to continue my search for Jolie to find some shit to wear.

I found her in her bedroom and got an outfit for the day. Of course Terrell's ass was still asleep so after knocking on his door and letting him know I would be out for the day me, Jolie and Saint headed out.

I went ahead and let Jolie ride shotgun while I hopped in the back. Saint gave me a sideways ass look, but since he wanted it to keep his distance that what I was gonna do too.

I was done chasing behind his ass and playing with fire when it came to him. We would just be cool ass homies from here on out, just like he wanted.

All sexual thoughts and feelings for him as my man were gonna be pushed out of mind until they really became out of mind.

It was time to focus on getting my shit together and making things happen. Despite the bad things that happened over the years, I still held on to hope and some dreams along the way.

Now that I was back home, and back with family I was gonna live that shit out and put in the hard work to finally make things go my way.

Saint

Damn man the shit with Nya couldn't have gone worse when I picked her and Jolie up this morning. I almost fucked up. On God shawty was lucky her ass wasn't pinned up against the wall taking the dick. I kept myself composed, after realizing what the fuck I was doing. But damn.

Nya was bad as fuck and her body was perfect from head to toe. I was a nigga after all so I fucking took my time looking at that shit. At least, I came to my senses and stopped shit before fucking her right in my sister's hallway.

I hoped I shut the shit down for good. I didn't wanna hurt Nya's feelings but it's the way it had to be for both of us. She seemed to accept it. I saw the look of defeat on her face even though she played shit off.

I wasn't trying to fuck around with her or take things as far as I did to begin with, but it was like I didn't have control over my actions for a minute.

Nya did some shit to me. It was all the way out of character for me. I was just gonna duck off after today and keep my distance from shawty.

Growing up Nya and me always said shit here and there, her more so than me. I always kept it light and acted like I wasn't interested. She never all out threw herself out there, just like I never tried to lead her on.

Even Jolie got in on the shit and used to clown me for being too overprotective of Nya. Buck didn't say shit, but he would give me a look and shake his head when I checked niggas for trying to holla at her.

After how close I came to fucking up, I had to do some drastic shit. I didn't play along this time. I rejected her straight out, hopefully for the last time. Now she could move on with her life without thinking I could ever be more to her than what I was.

We had a complicated ass relationship to say the least. Back in the day her ass would always act like my girl and I never stopped that shit. We were together minus all the physical shit. If any hoe tried to step to me or nigga to her when we were together, than we deaded the shit on sight.

Nya was really playing it cool between us too. It was awkward as hell the whole fucking day. Shit was never like this when we were around each other before.

I was getting to see a whole other side to her. She wasn't walking beside me or giving me those sexy ass looks that I expected to get.

She was giving all her attention to Jollie's ass. She kept her distance and even stayed ahead of me, not even looking my way unless it was when I was paying for their shit.

I didn't mind paying, shit I wanted to pay. I always took care of the both of them from the first day I started hustling. So there wouldn't be any other way the shit would go. But I wasn't feeling the cold shoulder shit.

After hours of shopping, the two of them were finally done. On the way back to my jeep, I happened to look over and see Smoke's whip a few rows over.

He was just getting out of his car, with some random bitch. This nigga kept different women with him for each day of the damn week. He stayed caught up in some dumb shit behind them. That shit couldn't have been me.

I kept all my moves behind closed doors. There never was a bitch on my arm that could claim a mothafucking thing about me. I didn't even believe in buying a bitch a meal let alone letting a bitch ride with me.

I didn't want to ever give them the wrong idea about what I wanted. To me it was a hundred percent about the pussy.

Smoke walked over to where we were, "Waaahhh" he said, nodding his head.

I greeted his ass back and noticed right away how all of his attention went to Nya. He didn't give a fuck about the bitch standing next to him or that Nya should have been off limits because she was with me. Even if she wasn't my woman, she was at this bitch with me.

From the look in his eyes it was gonna be a fucking problem. He was eyeing her up and down like I wasn't standing next to her. I took a step closer to her.

When I looked over at Nya, she actually had a look of interest back. I swear to God I was ready to drag her ass away from the nigga and make sure she understood there wasn't any way shit was about to go that way.

He must have forgotten lil' baby he had with him. She came up to where we were all standing and made her presence known.

"Okay, daaaaddddy I'm ready." She said wrapping her arm in his and kissing on his neck like we weren't all standing out in a damn parking lot. She was the extra thirsty type of bitch.

Don't get me wrong, I was fine with all that public shit. I would fuck a bitch wherever, whenever I saw fit. But it was obvious she was fronting and being extra because she was intimidated by Jolie and Nya. There was always insecure bitches when they were around.

Smoke shook the bitch off and stepped over in front of where Nya was standing, holding two of her shopping bags. He reached for her bags and asked to help put them in my ride.

Smoke was my nigga and had been loyal so far, but the shit he was doing was not happening. He knew I wasn't the type of nigga to wife a bitch. That alone should let him know she was off limits. For her to be out with me and Jolie meant she wasn't to be fucked with. That shit spoke volumes.

He was being real fucking disrespectful. I bet anything his ass recognized her from the other night out in Houston as the same woman I dragged out the club.

I never got into my personal shit with my niggas and the only person on my team that I ever spoke about anything with was Buck, not this nigga.

But he should know better than what the fuck he was doing. Since he didn't, some shit was gonna be taken care of later. No mothafucka disrespected me right out without me handling it.

"Nah, She good lil brudda." I said intercepting his attempt to step to Nya.

I went ahead and grabbed the two bags she had outstretched for him to help her with. I put them in the backseat of the jeep. I'm sure that both Jolie and Nya knew from my tone and demeanor I was ready to body this nigga.

Smoke's bitch ass even had the fucking nerve to look at me sideways like he had some more shit to say. He was smart enough to rethink saying another fucking word.

"This you partna?" He asked still being relentless in his pursuit of NyAsia.

"The fuck you mean? I said she good, ya heard." I said again, feeling my temper rise along with my voice.

This mothafucka was on some other shit, and all over a bitch he didn't' even fucking know. Now to me Nya wasn't just some bitch. But to him that was all she was. He didn't know shit about her and he wouldn't either.

So the fact that he was really questioning me out in the open about this shit and being persistent let me know there was more to his real motives.

I never thought he was on some snake shit, but it's little things you have to look out for. A sour ass attitude or overstepping a nigga's place were some of the things that always put the red flags up for me. So far Smoke had been nothing but loyal. But money and bitches, like my team was seeing was enough to cause a mothafucka to switch up in a heartbeat.

I was gonna watch his ass even closer from here on out. He didn't even fucking know me the way he thought he did for him to be coming at me wrong on this shit dealing with Nya.

I nodded my head. He finally got the fucking message that I was done talking and ready to head out. After the girls got in my jeep, he tried to play shit off and slapped hands with me, spitting some weak ass apology, about how it was his "bad" and he "didn't mean shit by it".

Yeah the nigga was trying his best to backtrack that shit, but his true feelings came out. I saw right through his ass.

Being close to Nya all day was one thing, but to be confronted with a nigga trying to holla at her, with me fucking standing by her side was a big ass pill to swallow.

Some shit had to change. I needed to put this shit to rest once and for all tonight and then somehow me and Nya would just have to move forward like family without the extra shit.

I had been thinking about this shit all day as I watched her walking around. I wanted her so bad that my eyes stayed locked on her fat ass swaying from side to side. My head was so fucked up over Nya, that I finally just said fuck it.

Maybe I was stuck on her so bad because she was the one I never had. If we got the shit out our systems, than it might be enough to get my head right. It was gonna have to be enough for me because right now I was caught up worrying about a bitch when my attention should have been on the shit I had going on in the streets.

So throughout the day I had been working on not only a plan to get Pedro and Martina off my back but for me to lay shit out for Nya tonight. If I gave in and fucked with her tonight, only one night, then we could go back to just being friends.

I was confident that she would still be willing to fuck with a nigga. I just had to get her to accept that we couldn't go further and would just to stay friends afterwards. Shit, maybe we could even fuck around from time to time.

The more I thought about the shit the more it seemed like the perfect fucking solution. That way I wouldn't be going back on the pledge I made to myself not to be tied down to a bitch and she could focus on her own shit.

While riding back to my sister's house I finally felt like I had a handle on the situation with both Nya and my plug. The shit with Pedro and his daughter was gonna be settled tomorrow. But now all my attention was on Nya.

The love I had for her was real but this physical shit was clouding my mind and that was some shit that got niggas killed out here.

Nya

I sat in the backseat of Saint's stupid ass jeep feeling pissed off. I was trying to keep my feelings from boiling over so I didn't go all the way off on this nigga and let him ruin the otherwise good ass day me and my best bitch had. But I swear on everything it was proving hard as fuck.

Back when we were both teenagers before I left, we always acted like a damn couple. It was our thing. Everybody knew that was just how we rolled. When I was younger, so many older bitches used to step to me about the shit. Of course me and Jolie always beat their asses and sent the hoes on their way.

They always went right back to Saint and complained about the shit like he was gonna check me or his sister on their behalf. All he would do was laugh at their ass and then give them the fucking boot for even trying some shit with me.

He never said we were together to anybody and he never said we weren't either. It was always confusing as fuck.

That was why I joked around with him the way I did. It was just natural. But when he went and got all serious with the shit and shut it down this morning it didn't feel like the innocent flirting like it was in the past anymore. My feelings were really out there different than they used to be.

I guess because I was older now, there was more at stake and I knew more about what real hurt and heartache felt like. The deep kind that was worse than this dumb in love shit. The kind where you feel like there is nothing for you, no love from anyone. So all you got is the little bit of love for yourself that you can muster up.

That last little bit of pride I felt was in jeopardy this morning with how he talked to me. So I closed down my own damn feelings too, or at least was determined to. It was time to put the childish ass ways and thinking behind me. I felt the real ass rejection that came out of his mouth.

So all day I made sure to keep my attention off that nigga and just focus on having a good ass time with my bestie. That shit worked too. Saint who????

Throughout the day, I didn't think about Saint's ass not one time in that way. I wouldn't let myself. One thing I was good at was taking my feelings out of shit when I needed to. I had grown accustomed to that shit from having to deal with pain, loss, terror all that and more. So this shit was nothing to me. No nigga would have power over my life, not even saint.

When that other man stepped to me in the parking lot, I wasn't really interested but he was good looking. He was dressed well and he was trying to help my ass out. So I was gonna let him.

It was clear that he and Saint knew each other so I didn't think he would get all funny acting about the shit either. It wasn't like I was trying to fuck the nigga out in the damn parking lot.

That shit quickly went south. Saint went and got all possessive and shit. Damn his ass was confusing as hell. I knew he thought that I needed to focus on getting my life together and I agreed with his ass on that topic. But, the shit in the parking lot wasn't nothing to me.

He should have just let it be and not blown it way up. I felt like he didn't have any respect for me to be a damn individual with my own mind. I had only been back one day and my head was all fucked up behind this man.

The frustration I was feeling was exhausting. I let out a deep breath, finally getting outside my head and thoughts, realizing that we were pulling back into Jolie's driveway.

Saint put the car in park and Jolie hopped out, closing the door behind her. Saint looked to me in the back seat, making eye contact through the rear view mirror. This shit was like déjà vu all over again from yesterday.

I continued to gather up the bags I had next to me and was about to pull on the door handle to get out, when this dumb ass nigga locked the damn door. I couldn't' even make this shit up if I wanted to.

I had no choice but to see what they hell his problem was now. It seemed like he was always giving me a damn talk and telling me about some shit he didn't agree with or like about me. I was fed the fuck up. Fuck Kwame "Saint" ....

"Nah shawty you comin' wit' me tonight." Saint said, still staring me down through the rear view mirror.

His voice made my pussy jump. I didn't have control over that shit if I wanted to, but I damn sure wasn't going there with his ass anymore either.

"Uh, uh. I'll pass on that. I appreciate today and I love you for everything you doin' but it's best if we just keep our distance, Don't you think? 'specially after this morning..." I said, looking back at his ass without an ounce of attitude in my voice.

I didn't want him to think I was in my feelings about the shit I was saying. I was good, or I would be good on his ass. There wasn't nothing in this world that I was gonna let hurt me. Damn sure not a man.

"No." He responded back before looking back up, trying to ignore the shit I was saying.

He put the car in reverse and drove off even though I didn't want to go anywhere with his ass. This man always had to have his way like a spoiled ass baby.

I texted Jolie to let her know what was up. The bitch responded with smiley emojis and shit, like she thought her brother kidnapping me was funny.

It only took a few minutes before he pulled into a similar driveway to Jolie's. The house we were parked in front of sat on a bigger lot than any other houses around. It was newer, one I'd never seen before. Saint was definitely doing the damn thing. His house was nice and clean on the outside but nothing over the top that would make it stand out for a hit.

I made up my mind on the short ass ride over that I was just gonna let Saint say what the fuck he wanted to say. I tried preparing myself for whatever it was. It didn't make sense that his ass couldn't just tell me before I got out of the car over at his sister's.

He usually didn't hold back from speaking his mind with me. Bringing me to his house, had my ass all worked up racking my brain, trying to figure out what he needed to tell me. Maybe he had a bitch or a even a child. It had to be something serious if he was trying to ease me into it.

Not that Saint owed me an explanation or a damn thing. What we had was beyond a relationship or anything he might tell me. We had a bond no matter what.

By the time I followed him into the house and sat down across from him in the living room, I was ready for whatever he was gonna lay on me. Or so I thought. But Saint never ceased to amaze me.

"Okay you got me over here so what's up? What you gotta tell me?" I asked once we were settled in. He handed me a bottle of water then sat down himself.

"I been thinkin' and shit... You always been mine, ya heard. But I'm not fittin' be tied down to no bitch. Not even you. We just need to get this shit out our systems then won't be no more tension." He laid the shit out like what he said made perfect damn sense.

I was at a loss. His words took my breath away and I didn't know how the hell I should respond. I took a drink of the water, then continued to sit there thinking about what he was saying. If I was understanding his ass right, he wanted to fuck and then keep shit cool between us.

Normally, I wouldn't even consider no shit like this especially since sex wasn't shit to me and I never felt the need for it. Don't get me wrong all the men I had been with enjoyed themselves, but I was never fully into it.

Truthfully, sitting here hearing Saint finally admit to wanting me the same way I wanted him and us having sex, did make me wonder what it would be like. If I agreed, I didn't want it to make shit worse or fuck up our friendship.

My silence made Saint even bolder with his proposition. He stood up and walked across the room to where I was. He bent forward, leaning over me, placing each his strong hands on my knees.

I hadn't given his ass an answer yet. I wanted to let him know that if I said yes, then I was gonna hold him to the shit he said too. He wanted it to be a one-time thing and nothing more. If I agreed, I wanted him to stand by that shit.

I was only considering this because my body wanted this nigga. He was the only man alive who ever made me feel this way.

I pulled back as much as possible to put some space between us. The way he was taking control and kissing me had me in a damn daze already.

"I'm down, but you gotta keep your word that this is it. This one time and that it won't change shit between us. I'm not gonna be one of those hoes you got chasing after you, so I don't expect to be treated like one... Don't change up on me. "I said while my breathing slowed back down.

"I'm a gangsta shawty, you got my word on that shit. Now you ready to get fucked good?"

He said that shit with a confidence that sent chills though my body. Then lifted me up in a single motion. I wrapped my legs around his waist while his hands gripped my ass, holding me up.

With our bodies in close contact, I felt his heart beating fast against my breasts through his shirt. We were really bout to do this.

Saint carried me up the steps and into his bedroom. The room was pitch black with the lights turned off. He set me down on the edge of bed. I was nervous as hell, trying to keep my composure. Was I really ready for this?

I still couldn't see shit because it was dark as hell. For some reason I wanted to see everything. I was always shy and liked the lights off before, but with Saint all my feelings were different. This was just one night. No strings attached, so I wanted to take it all in.

He turned on the lights to a dim setting and then came back over to where I was. I laid back on the bed and pulled my shirt off. He came to the edge of the bed, and grabbed my legs lifting them up, spreading them apart on either side of him. He pulled me down towards him and lifted my ass up in the air, undoing my jeans, taking them off.

He started licking and kissing my legs from my calves to my thighs. As he made his way up, my pussy started throbbing wanting more and more of his touch and tongue, all of him.

He paused and slid his jeans off in the process. He was down to just his boxers. Saint's body was intimidating as hell. This nigga was fucking perfect. He was strong as hell with a chiseled six pack. Even his tattoos turned me on.

He had a set of initials on his chest. I sat up and leaned in closer to read them. I saw Jolie's first then looked to the other side where mine were. I ran my hand over the tattoo of my initials and started kissing his chest. Then worked my way down.

I got caught up for in the moment, my emotions getting the best of me, seeing the tattoo of my initials. This shit was gonna be harder than I thought. We were already in way deeper than we admitted. But there was not turning back now.

When I made it to the waistband of his boxers, I pulled them down and grabbed ahold of his dick. I swear to God this nigga had my ass paralyzed. I didn't know what the fuck I was gonna do with his big ass dick.

I wanted to please him, and I knew how to give head but damn I had never seen a dick this big or fucked a nigga with some shit like this.

I sat there with his hard dick in my face, my mouth and pussy watering and couldn't fucking move.

"I'ma teach you how to handle the dick shawty, now get on the bed." He said taking control.

"Saint…"

"Get on the bed". He said again, with more bass in his voice. Giving me that sexy ass look, daring me to defy him.

I got up and sat my ass on the bed like he said. If he hadn't spoke up, I might've just said fuck it and changed my mind. I wanted to do this with Saint. I wanted to make him feel good as hell, I just wasn't confident that I was gonna be able to fuck and suck him the way all those other bitches he fucked with did.

I was an amateur compared to most women my age. He might have thought I was out there like that, but I wasn't.

He came towards me and turned me around rough as hell. Saint was a fucking boss and that shit was coming through now.

I played right along and got on all fours, then reached down to my pussy and began playing in it. Giving him a full view of my perfectly shaved pussy from the back. He wasn't moving fast enough, so I looked back over my shoulder, but I wish the fuck I hadn't.

His dick was just too damn big. I started to tell him again that it wasn't gonna fit, that my pussy couldn't take it. As much as I wanted to fuck Saint and take it there with him, I really didn't think I could.

Shit I was scared as hell now. I tried to move so I could face him, but Saint wasn't having that shit either.

Before I could object again, he put the tip at my entrance and pushed himself in. He knew me enough to know when I was scared and this nigga wasn't trying to let me back out.

"Ahhhhhh, Saint, szzzzz, damn." I screamed out. I felt like his dick was tearing me apart.

He stopped working himself in and remained still, letting me adjust to his size.

"Ease up. Let me in and throw that shit back." He said into my ear from behind.

He leaned his body into mine with his hands gripping my hips.

His voice did the damn trick and my pussy responded just like he wanted. He slid the mothafucka all the way in causing my whole body to shake and my juices to gush out more, coating his dick.

I couldn't even fucking make a sound. No nigga ever made me cum right away like this. That shit was crazy as hell.

Once Saint worked himself all the way in, he began going to work, digging in deeper than I thought possible. I really couldn't take the shit so I moved up, as far into the headboard as I could. All that did was make him grab ahold of my hips and pull me back into him so he could fuck me the way he wanted.

I couldn't form a coherent thought the way he was fucking me. My body was shaking. But I couldn't move or fuck him back. The shit hurt so bad, but also felt like the best feeling in the damn world.

He was working my ass out for real. He slowed up the pace while I let out the biggest orgasm of my life. I thought his ass was done too, but I was wrong.

Instead he pulled out and then gripped my ass hard as hell with both hands. He spread me wide and spit in between my ass cheeks. Then started working his fingers in and out of my pussy.

The shit felt so good that I began bouncing my ass and squeezing my pussy muscles on his fingers, while he watched. Shit, he was gonna make me cum from finger fucking me.

I was so tight from him gripping my ass, that it was almost hurting and sending me over the edge.

Then he fucked up my whole world, when he put his mouth on my pussy from the back, licking and sucking on me like I had never felt before.

My body gave in again to his touch and mouth and I began grinding against his face trying to let him taste every fucking thing I had to give. My body tensed up getting close to another climax, but he stopped eating my pussy right before I could cum.

My breathing was heavy as hell and I was about to pass out from what he was doing to me. He had me ready to tap out.

"Now turn that ass around. Let me see my pussy bust."

Him talking nasty to me gave me the energy to keep going. I turned around. Saint lifted both of my legs in the air in a V, then brought my pussy up to the tip of his dick.

Watching the way he fucked me was some other shit. The way he was handling my body was like he knew every damn spot I didn't even know I had.

Our eyes met as he slid the rest of the way in.

"You betta take the dick, if you want it."

I still didn't respond. I couldn't. My breath was still taken from how deep he was going. I felt every inch all the way in my stomach. The way he filled me up made me want more and more even though I really couldn't move from the shit.

"Say that shit."

This nigga really stopped fucking me and took the time to give me that serious ass face he always did when he was on some straight bullshit. His stubborn ass needed to go ahead and put the dick back in and make me cum again.

I couldn't help but to smile at him and let him hear what he wanted to hear. More than anything, I wanted him to start fucking me again. Any and every way he wanted, I was gonna take the damn dick.

"I love your dick damn. Now fuck me!" I said.

Then I went ahead and grabbed his shit and put it back in myself. My body missed the feeling of him being inside me already.

As soon as the words left my mouth, he went back to work.

My body was starting to adjust to his size and I was finally able to move enough to start throwing the pussy back at him. I worked my hips from underneath and let my mind go and the feelings take over.

"Oh my GOD, SAINT! I moaned.

He reached down and cupped both my breasts hard, squeezing them. Then leaned into my neck, locking my ass in place. This nigga was laying the dick on me and tearing me up but I didn't want him to stop.

"I'm bout to cum, hold that shit in and cum with me."

"Yes, daddy".

He moved his hands to grip my ass from underneath. I felt his body tense up too. He took a few more long deep strokes, causing us both to cum at the same time.

He stayed laid up in my pussy, still inside me for a good five minutes. Even though I couldn't really handle Saint's dick or the way he fucked me, I did something to his ass too. My pussy had his ass like he had me.

He rolled over still inside of me, pulling me on top of him. I was now on top straddling him. I felt his dick getting hard again while he looked up at me and began rubbing my breasts and kissing my forearm. Paying attention to every part of my body.

I didn't know if I would be able to walk in the morning but I wanted more. I wanted all I could get from his ass. Since this was all he was offering I was gonna make it worth it.

Jolie

If you asked me, my brother and best friend were destined to be together. They just didn't want to admit the shit to themselves. Nya always followed behind his ass and as we got older he started looking at her different too.

Me, Nya, Buck and my brother were all fucked up by our past in some way. If those two out of the group could get their shit together and have a real relationship than that meant there was hope for me too. Plus they deserved happiness.

Nya came up different than us. Her parents weren't like ours. They didn't take off and leave their kids. They worked every day and didn't spend much time at home, but the love was there.

I remember what it was like going over to Nya's house for holidays and shit. Her parents lived a quiet life. They stayed to themselves and didn't do shit like the other people in the neighborhood.

I used to think about what it would be like if she was my real sister and they were my parents. As a little girl all I wanted was to feel loved. I didn't get that shit from anyone outside of my brother. He was the only father I ever knew.

When her parents got killed that shit fucked up any illusion I had of happy endings. It seemed like bad shit was an inevitable part of life.

Nya's parents weren't buried like most people. Their bodies were burned in the car wreck when it exploded. So their remains were put into some containers and then kept in one of those above ground burials in the cemetery.

The whole funeral was so weird. It was like some shit I'd never seen. Her father's family were really the only people in attendance but only a few of them actually came. Nobody spoke more than a few words to each other. It was just real different than what I witnessed at the couple funerals I'd been to.

I thought shit was funny back then the way her missing aunt just all the sudden showed up out of the blue on the same day as the funeral too, but what could I say. It all happened so fast and before me or Saint even knew Nya had left, she was long gone.

We had no clue Nya's aunt was gonna take her away that same night and we wouldn't see her again. She was waiting for me at my house one minute and then gone when I got back.

My brother told me that she needed some time alone after the hard day she had. I thought there was more to it since he sounded funny as hell when he told me how she just up and left. It wasn't like Nya to back down or to take off without at least waiting to tell me herself. She was always considerate about everything. I was the reckless one.

After she left, it was it felt like my best friend didn't want shit to do with me and turned her back on me just like everybody else did in my life, besides my brother.

It really hurt me, since I loved her like a sister. After months passed, and her ass didn't call me, not even one time I grew more and more pissed at her.

I went through the past 10 years believing she fucked me over. I wasn't into trusting mothafuckas and I wasn't close to hardly anyone. Just like my brother, I was fucked up behind being abandoned and shit. I could at least admit it, but his ass acted like the way he lived was perfectly normal.

Now that Nya told me about what kept her from getting in touch with me, I felt at peace with it. The minute she stepped out of my brother's car, it was like old times. How could I be mad, when she went through hell. I heard the hurt in her voice and with the tears flowing down her cheeks, my anger subsided.

I felt bad for spending all these years questioning her as my friend. Even though we both grew up and lived life apart for so long, there was no denying that our friendship was the same. Neither one of our personalities was any different either.

I hoped with time Nya could trust me enough and let me all the way in. She still didn't get into details about what happened to her. The only way a person can truly heal is to face the demons of their past. Nya was strong as hell and I knew one day she would be ready to face hers.

I really hoped my brother didn't fuck with her feelings tonight. Whatever was going on, they needed to come to some kind of understanding. Today was awkward as hell between the two of them.

As much as I loved my bestie, I was also relieved that she was gone tonight. It gave me a minute to handle my own situation that I got myself into.

Me and Buck had a thing going on for over a year now, well it was actually a long time coming, but neither one of us acted on our feelings until then. There were always the looks and the sly ass remarks we both made about who the other was with. But now my feelings for Buck were real.

I wanted to come clean and let my brother know that we were together. But he was on some other shit.

So over the last couple months I started acting out, trying to get the nigga to come to his senses. I would go to the club with one or two home girls and dance with whoever dared to approach me and looked good enough.

Every single time Buck ended up showing up and showing the fuck out. Then afterward we would argue about the shit and have a big ass fight, just to turn around and end up fucking. Having some good 'ol make up sex.

We had gotten into a bad cycle and I was tired of the shit. Going out and acting desperate for a man's attention wasn't me.

For a week straight I ignored Buck each time he attempted to get in contact with me. All the phone calls, the texts, and the voicemails he left trying to get me to give him a chance to make things right. I just wasn't feeling none of that shit. I was way too grown for what he was willing to offer me.

No matter how serious my feelings were for him, I was ready to really be done with his ass and move on. He ended up showing up to my job this past Friday afternoon. He parked right next to my car in the schoolhouse parking lot.

I still tried to ignore him, but he got out of his car and stood in front of my door so I couldn't get in. Buck knew I wasn't gonna create a scene because I loved my job. So I had to listen to his ass like he wanted.

I agreed to meet him sometime this weekend to talk.

So far I hadn't made time for his ass. With Nya here it was a good ass distraction and helped me avoid dealing with him. But one thing I believed in and he knew about me was that when I gave my word, that shit was bond. I felt like if you could break your word about even the smallest thing then you weren't shit, simple as that.

I told Terrell that I was heading out and to hit me or Nya up if he needed anything. I already had him program my number in his phone. Then I texted Buck to let him know I was on the way over. He only lived on the other side of the hood anyway.

We all still stayed close together. No matter how deep my brother and Buck got into the drug game shit hadn't changed much for us, except how much money we had.

I prepared myself for the conversation I was about to have. I knew and admitted willingly that I loved Buck. The problem was that he had such a fucked up childhood. I mean way worse than me and Saint. He didn't know how to take the love I was giving him or return it.

He opened up to me about so much shit, but if he wasn't willing to make things official and really claim my ass, then I had no choice but to leave him alone. Tonight would either be the end or the beginning for us.

Saint

When I woke up and felt Nya next to me it was some crazy ass shit. What the fuck did I do...

Damn, her pussy was better than any other bitch I ever fucked with. But I should have expected that. Everything about Nya was perfect to me.

Last night was some shit I would never forget. But I still meant what I said. I wasn't gonna fuck up our real ass friendship and the love we had for each other end of story. I was a dog ass nigga and still believed she deserved better than what I could give her. So it was only right if I fell back and let shawty go.

I was a father's worst nightmere. The nigga they never wanted their daughter meet. I didn't pretend to be something I wasn't. Not one time did I develop feelings for a bitch I was fucking. Even if one of them thought she could change me, she was dead ass wrong. I just wasn't built like that. I had bitches in rotation to satisfy my needs but I wasn't about to go back on the shit I believed in.

With Nya it was different. I Knew I loved her ass. There wasn't a doubt in my damn mind. But I wasn't what she needed and honestly, I didn't want to be.

I waited to wake her up until after I got out of the shower and was already dressed. I playfully started shaking her shoulders back and forth, talking shit to her the whole time.

"Dick got you in a coma." I said loud still trying to wake her ass up. She grumbled something as she turned over and put her face in the pillow, still trying to avoid waking up.

"Get yo' ass up. We both got shit to do." I said and then slapped her on her bare ass. She did that shit to herself turning over and thinking I wasn't gonna touch the mothafucka. It didn't matter that we weren't gonna fuck around again. Nya was still sexy as hell and her ass was all out in full view.

I was tempted to get back undressed and slide up in her pussy one more time as I watched her ass shake from the impact of the slap.

Seeing Nya's beautiful body in my bed partially wrapped in my white Egyptian sheets was a sight to fucking see. I took the time to look her body over one more time. I was gonna miss this shit. Having her ready and willing to do whatever the fuck I wanted and take the dick any way I wanted like she did last night.

Nya said some more shit under her breath that I couldn't make out, but I already knew she was cursing my ass out. She finally sat up and really started talking shit back to my ass. I was relieved that it seemed like things were still the same between us. She wasn't in her feelings and shit wasn't fucked up between us despite what we just did.

"Whatever nigga. Your ass the one tapped out the last time. It's your fault with that mothafucka! My walk gon' be fucked up!" She said before giving me a big ass grin.

"That's what your ass gets for wanting the dick so bad shawty." I said laughing at how serious she looked.

Nya got up and took a few steps. "Ughhh, I hate you nigga." She replied and then picked up a pillow and threw that shit at me.

I tossed her one of my Ts and some joggers she could put them on after she washed up. She grabbed them midair and began walking towards the bathroom. She really did have a fucked up walk, walking all bowlegged and taking light steps.

Every step she took today she would think about fucking me. I couldn't even lie, I loved that shit. I was glad she ain't never been with a nigga like me.

Once I heard the shower running, I stepped out of the room and made my way downstairs.

I needed to drop Nya off and get shit settled for the sit down with Pedro. The meeting was only two hours away. I wore my wheat colored custom Timbs, some dark jeans and a simple Supreme black Tee today. I wasn't a flashy nigga. All my shit was fresh, clean and top of the line, but I didn't advertise my bank account. Any nigga that tried to outdo his position went down as fast as he came up.

As my shit grew and our business increased so did the amount of shit I owned. With this Houston setup, I might consider getting a new home out of the hood and upgrading some other shit.

I had a couple million in cash on hand at any time, and more dough invested. But I needed to make sure my supply and daily sales surpassed my day to day living before I switched anything up.

Even if I ever got to the point where I had a billion dollars, I would keep my moves on the low. It was just who I was. Only broke niggas bragged about the shit they had. Real niggas on that true gangsta shit kept their fucking lips sealed about every fucking thing. Wasn't no bragging happening on my end ever.

Martina kept hitting my line nonstop the whole damn weekend. I had to turn the shit off last night. I wouldn't disrespect Nya over another hoe. When I turned my phone back on this morning, she hadn't called again. Maybe the bitch got the message, but more than likely she knew I was about to meet up with her pops.

For all I knew Martina could've already told his ass some shit. She was the type of bitch to spew lies and make shit more than what it was to show me she could, just because her feelings were hurt. So I was going into this shit expecting Pedro to want me dead.

Pedro had been my plug since I started moving heavy weight years ago. I knew how his ass thought and operated giving me an advantage. He was gonna try and intimidate me and play games like he always did. That would give me enough time to leverage his ass.

There were two reasons he was gonna let me and my niggas walk out of there alive today. I was the only mothafucka with the capabilities to run Houston right now. Killing me, meant losing out on money while he got another nigga to work his way up.

Even a cartel boss couldn't pull strings in the streets and pick a nigga to take over. That shit had to be earned from the street level up. On top of that, I knew some shit that his ass was gonna want to hear.

I've had my back against the wall a hundred times before and always came out of that shit standing tall. Shit like this came with the territory and I wasn't backing down. It was what it was.

Me, Buck and Smoke single handedly took down Pedro's competition in Houston. The hit ended up being real beneficial to my operation all the way around. We got good ass intel along with gaining some of the shit that the niggas left behind.

When we went out there, we flipped half the niggas on the team I was now taking over in a few days' time. It was too much just to come in and try and kill all the mothafuckas on his team. Shit would have never worked if we moved that sloppy.

I planted a worker on their team six months ago. He put in some real ass work. After a month of joining up with them, he started to make moves. He got in everyone's ears about how fucked up their boss was treating them and let them know there was a new and improved nigga ready to step in and take over.

He didn't come right out and say the shit, but he took small opportunities to drop hints. Of course there were still some loyal niggas that didn't want to bite the hand that fed them. I respected that shit, but it didn't save their lives. It was either fall in line or get laid the fuck out.

As soon as word made it to the crew that I was in town and ready to step in, my man on the inside made shit happen. To tell the truth, he did most of the leg work before my ass touched down. He was the fucking truth and earned himself a damn promotion for all the work he put in. What he accomplished singlehandedly was more than most mothafuckas could do with a team of niggas behind them.

The old boss's team took each other out, making shit that much easier for me. The ones left standing after the bullets stopped flying were ready to work under me.

My man took out the boss with a bullet to the head but left his second in command alive. He was smart as hell for that shit. He said that his right hand might know something useful and he was right.

Me and Buck were able to get information out of him before we put him out his misery. There wasn't shit for the nigga to hold out for. His boss was already dead, so it wasn't selling out. In order to keep his family safe he sang like a fucking bird.

We found out who their connect was and how to get in contact with him. The nigga also told us where their stash was. But the real icing on the cake was when he gave up the name of the man that murdered Pedro's brother.

That was the reason the two cartels went to war and were at odds with each other in the first place. It was a blood feud that went back 20 years. The name and location of the person responsible for Pedro's brother's death was my ticket out of the fucked up spot I was in.

If Pedro couldn't look past me fucking his daughter and didn't want to do business with me anymore, I was fine with that shit. Over the years I only kept fucking with him on the strength of loyalty and because of the CCC agreement in my city. The way he operated and the fuck shit he always tried to pull had me ready to say fuck him too.

There were times when he shorted my bread or tried to do some other shit to show his power instead of just being a straight up mothafucka. A real fucking boss didn't have to prove how much power they had. Their actions proved who the fuck they were.

I planned on getting in contact with the same cartel he was up against. Fuck it, with them backing me the mothafucka couldn't come back and touch me after he got the name of who was responsible.

I needed to stay ten steps ahead of the Pedro. To the Mexican cartels, every nigga in the states and their whole team were disposable. I didn't fool myself thinking otherwise.

After Nya finished getting ready I dropped her off at Jolie's, then headed to the safe house I kept downtown for meetings. I crossed over the bridge ready for this shit to get over with sooner than later. Buck already rounded up the lieutenants and we needed to go over some shit before the meeting. Nobody on our team under them knew about the safe house. I only put niggas in charge of shit after they put in enough work to earn the shit.

Most of my team saw me as a cold ass nigga who was as deadly as I was serious about my business. I knew my reputation, and I purposefully made niggas fear me when I was younger. Now I just didn't give a fuck either way. I was an OG and wasn't new to none of this street shit. I didn't need to prove a damn thing to a soul.

But nobody working under me could say they didn't eat good or weren't treated right. I wasn't trying to build friendships and shit. All I needed was the money and the respect that came with my position. I compensated my team fairly.

That didn't stop a few pussy ass niggas from making their way into my camp over the years. Every fucking time I cut that shit off at the head. That's why me and Buck were still the niggas in charge of the West Bank.

I parked in front of the safe house and checked my phone one more time. I almost expected to see a call or text from Nya. But she hadn't hit me up.

I laid the dick on her last night and lil baby was gonna be fucked up behind that shit for a minute. When Nya looked at my dick up close and personal, I knew her ass was gonna try and back out, but I didn't let her second guess her decision. With her butt naked in my bed, shit was a done deal and I made sure to leave my mark on her pussy.

Me and Nya fucking was some fate shit. Wasn't no pussy like hers and I could tell right away shawty hadn't been around. That was fine with me though, I taught her ass all types of shit last night. I thought about calling her ass to see what she was up to, but decided against that shit.

I needed to keep focused on the shit that was about to go down. The meeting with Pedro was only an hour away and I had to make sure my backup was on point and ready to lay mothafuckas out at any time. I wasn't trying to die. But I damn sure was gonna be prepared for the shit.

I walked inside and was greeted by Buck, Smoke and three of the other niggas that ran my spots. Smoke gave me a head nod and his usual smile like shit was all good between us. As far as he needed to know everything was good. I peeped that hoe shit, and planned to weed it out of him.

I ran the plan down to everybody. They were going to follow behind me and Buck. We would be outnumbered but it was enough pressure without sending off any kind of warning to Pedro. Just to let him know there was some shit that would pop off if he tried to take me out.

We were in and out of the safe house in less than 30 minutes. The plan was straightforward, but foolproof with multiple scenarios. We all headed out at the same time.

Buck hopped in my BMW 650. This bitch was my fucking baby. It sat clean as fuck all platinum and chrome. I had the shit delivered last week, ready to go.

This wasn't my usual day to day ride. But I decided to pull the mothafucka out today. When it came to business shit, everything down to the clothes a nigga wore said something about the type of business he conducted. How you carried yourself said a lot about who the fuck you were.

"Damn bruh, this shit smooth." Buck said once he was sitting in the passenger seat.

"Says the nigga that don't wanna spend a fucking dime on shit." I said back, joking with his ass.

"Pass me that." I said, reaching for the blunt of the loud he just lit up.

The meeting was downtown in the French quarter at a restaurant that I hadn't been to before. I didn't even go down there often because it was filled with tourists and shit. All the old spots were gone with the flooding. Now it was like a foreign ass country inside the city limits.

It only took a few minutes and we were pulling into the busy ass streets that were filled with people visiting.

Once I spotted the restaurant I drove past it and went around the block, before I doubled back and pulled into one of the few empty spots across the street. The restaurant looked like a regular ass bar and grill, nothing special.

I stepped out of the car and walked over to the trunk. Buck followed suit and met me at the back of the car. He was ready to take care of the shit like I was.

I had a compartment installed by one of the niggas in Baton Rouge that did custom shit. I didn't want niggas around my city to know shit about my moves.

The compartment was under the spare tire and it concealed an area big enough for a few choppas to be held out of view. I didn't ride dirty with drugs anymore. I had runners for that shit, but I needed to keep some heat close at hand.

Since I was a convicted felon all these pistols could get me some big ass digits in Fed time. I tried to stay the fuck under the radar, but either way I wasn't gonna go into a meeting like this unprepared.

I knew that I wouldn't be allowed near Pedro with any tools on me. But my team could hold their shit from a distance.

I reached in and took out the 38 Smith and Wesson and handed it over to Buck. The rest of my niggas had their own shit. Buck tucked that it into the back of his pants and then unzipped his bomber jacket. His crazy ass reached in and grabbed ahold of an AR he already had on him. Yeah this nigga wasn't playing. If these Mexican mothafuckas started with the shit, then it was gonna be some bodies dropping on their end.

Smoke and the others came over to where we stood. I closed the trunk and started walking over towards the entrance of the restaurant. Nobody said a word. Every one of us knew that walking in here could be us walking into a trap. This was life or death every fucking day so it wasn't shit to niggas like us.

I opened the door and walked inside. A hostess greeted us. She didn't look surprised to see me or the entourage behind me.

Without asking me anything, she turned around and led me and my team through restaurant.

We followed her towards the back of the room on the first floor, where she opened two sliding doors that led to a big ass room made for larger parties.

Even though it was the middle of the day, the restaurant kept the lights low, giving the feeling of night.

Two of Pedro's goons came over to where I was as soon as the doors closed behind us. They patted me down and then let me walk over to the table at the far side of the room.

I pulled out the chair next to Pedro and sat down on his side since he was at the head of the table.

The rest of my team stayed posted by the door with their hands ready and their stances showing them to be the thorough ass niggas they were.

Even Smoke wasn't a bitch made nigga, he was just a snake. His ass had a purpose for now, but it was gonna be a different story when the time came.

Pedro didn't greet me with the same warm greeting he usually did, so I didn't feel the need to say shit to his ass either. I could already tell Martina got in his ear from the way he was acting.

"So what was so important that you needed to meet with me right away?" He asked in his Spanish accent.

"I'm not gonna bullshit you. I been close to Martina and I wanna keep shit professional from here on out. No disprespect. I wanted to come to you and tell you man to man. I also wanted see about moving forward with the Houston deal." I said keeping shit short and sweet.

It was what it was at this point. The man was either gonna try to off my ass, come at me later, or let shit slide. I wasn't hiding behind a bitch any more.

I hadn't told him about all the information I had. I wanted to see what his real intentions were first so I knew what my next move was gonna be. His reaction would tell me everything I needed know.

"Fuck you! Dirty ass nigger, touching my daughter! How dare you!" Pedro's dumb ass yelled out. Spitting on me in the process. Then he reached his arm out, trying to grab me by the back of the head.

Plug or not, Cartel boss or not, I wouldn't go out like a bitch or let another man alive put his hands on me like I was one. He already disrespected me with his words and his nasty ass spit.

So when his hand touched the back of my head, my instincts kicked in and I threw a solid ass punch. I rocked the mothafucka even while I was sitting the fuck down. The entire room erupted with guns drawn and both sides yelling shit at each other.

Somehow everybody kept their composure enough that no guns were discharged. Even without full force, Pedro was fucked up from the blow I laid on him. I felt my knuckles split from the damn impact alone. He was still in his seat, leaned up against the shit looking dazed the fuck out.

I pushed my chair back and stood to my feet, looking down at his ass and using the napkin to wipe my shirt where his spit landed.

To me he was pitiful. To let a nigga like me come in here and boss the fuck up on him should have never fucking happened with the power he should have had. I should be dead right now. But his weakness was my gain.

I looked him square in the eyes and told his bitch ass what the fuck was about to happen now.

"It ain't goin down like that. Now this what the fuck fittin' to happen, I handle Houston without a fucking problem, ya heard. Then you'll get the name of the person responsible for your brother's death, but not before that shit happen. And from here on out your hoe ass daughter ain't got shit to do with my mothafuckin' business."

Pedro sat there glaring up at my ass, but he didn't' say shit until I turned around and had my back to him. Yeah he was a fucking bitch.

"You think I'm gonna let you live after this? You're dead!" He shouted at my back.

All I did was look back and smile like he said some shit I liked. Fuck, I kind of did. I knew he thought I should be fearful of making an enemy of him, but that shit gave me a rush. His ass should have feared me and he didn't even realize it.

See the thing about a nigga like me, is fear don't exist. With him, that's the only shit he knows. I came up from the gutta and dying wasn't shit to me. Being a bitch wasn't an option in my life.

All his ass knew was the best of everything. He was scared of losing everything. I been at the bottom and you couldn't fear falling if you already felt the ground before.

I opened the sliding doors to the room and walked out the bitch like I came in, untouched. My niggas were right there with their shit still out until Buck closed the doors and all of my team put their heat away. We already planned this shit out to a fucking "T" and figured they would hold the meeting in a room without cameras. Now out in the main part of the restaurant, there was no telling and almost every nigga on my team had some kind of record. Wasn't too many niggas true to the game that didn't. If a nigga didn't have any run ins with the law, they most likely were a snitch or hadn't done enough shit yet to get caught up.

I hopped back in my BMW and put that shit in drive. We all drove off in different directions, each headed our own way. It was time for the others to get back to their posts and run the traps. I couldn't emphasize hard work enough. My team was the hardest workers on these fucking blocks in New Orleans. They worked hard and the shit paid off, wasn't no days off in the trap.

I pulled back up to the house uptown where we met before the meeting. Buck's car was parked a street over from the safe house. Before he got out I wanted to fill him in on the shit I peeped yesterday with Smoke.

Every fucking move we made out here, we did together. Buck only tolerated Smoke because he proved to be loyal over the years, and I vouched for him. I was the one who brought him into this shit for real.

"I think lil brudda on some snake shit." I said.

"That shit ain't no surprise. When you wanna handle it?" He asked always ready to kill a mothafucka. Buck was crazy as hell. But my ass wasn't too far behind.

"I'm gonna see what he got goin' on first. We need to see how far shit goes." I answered, referring to the rat shit that was now a part of our team. I needed to see if he was on some real foul ass shit and if so, who else was in on it with him. I wanted to cut off the head of the snake then the body would die. But I needed to know who the fuck the body was.

I finished with, "Keep a lookout."

"Word." Buck said back.

Buck seemed more off than usual. His ass was never a talker, but he usually would follow up with more shit than just a single word, especially when it was some serious shit like this.

I wasn't sweating it though, if it was some shit he wanted to get off his chest or needed to talk through, then he knew I was his partna through and through.

He nodded his head and opened the door to get out. After he was gone and in his own car, I pulled off. I wanted to get back home and prepare for the trip I needed to take back to Houston. The ride to Houston wasn't that long but I was gonna catch a flight this time. I had to be in and out, back and forth without all that wasted drive time.

This expansion was the new beginning I was looking for. I loved my hometown, but I wanted more. I was a hungry ass nigga and couldn't get enough of the bread or the challenge the game gave me.

Houston was exactly what I was looking for. I could focus on my business shit and keep my distance from Nya in the process. It was a win win.

Nya

It had been two days since my damn sex fest. Yes I called it a sex fest and I was glad as hell that I went through with it and got that shit out my system.

Over the past couple days, my mind wandered back to Saint from time to time. But now that I knew him intimately I felt like I could really move forward and stop being all caught up with wondering. A whole lot of fucking wondering.

Jolie went back to work yesterday and today I was getting on my own grind. I didn't have my car but Saint dropped off an all black Mercedes Sunday night with a note that didn't say shit, other than my damn name. That was just like his ass, to not give a person a chance to reject what the fuck he had to say or what gift he had to give.

I couldn't lie though, the shit was bad as hell and I was loving the newfound freedom I had. It was like my whole life was on the upswing changing for the better.

I went and enrolled Terrell's ass in school right away Monday morning. This morning I dropped him off too. He tried to play like he didn't want to be some new kid in town. Even though he didn't like the shit, he would get over it. Because his ass was most definitely going to damn school.

Terrell was a good student anyway, no matter how much he tried to play shit off. He cared about his grades and his image just the same. I was proud of how he was turning out. It was the one thing that I had gotten somewhat right over the years where I was responsible for him, and I was gonna stay right on his ass too.

I wasn't pressed to find a job or do anyhing really. I knew I could depend on Saint and Jolie for as long as I needed. But that shit just wasn't me.

So today I drove over to the community college. I thought about getting my GED for the longest. I hoped I passed the shit, so I could start taking some basic college courses. I heard that after you got your associates, even with a GED, you could go ahead on to a regular University.

It would be a dream come true to actually be able to pursue my lifetime goal of becoming a lawyer. That was what I used to plan on becoming.

I remember telling Saint that one day I would keep his ass out of jail and be the hood lawyer that helped out all the homies. That shit may have sounded like wishful thinking now, but when I was a kid I was determined to make that shit happen. Then life happened and I had to give up on all that shit.

Now I wasn't so sure I would go through with all that, but I was definitely gonna be educated at least having my GED so I could get a decent ass job. Maybe not a top paying one, but some entry level position.

I finished at the college and started driving around trying to find a job. I headed over to the corner store to pick up a newspaper. I searched online for jobs, but around here it seemed like most jobs were still posted in the newspaper.

As I stood up from leaning over and picking up the paper, I got a feeling of someone behind me. I instantly knew it was a man.

Whenever a nigga was close I always felt their presence even if I didn't see their ass. I constantly had to keep my guard up for 10 years in case some mothafucka tried some shit.

I didn't always live in the apartment that me and Saint just burned down. I was in a whole lot of fucking worse spots than that place. Too many men, tried too many times, to take advantage of me. That's how I ended up becoming a beast with the blades. I kept those shit on me at all times.

I turned around ready to talk shit to whoever felt the need to be up in my personal space. But when I did, it ended up being the same nigga we ran into the other day at the mall.

So instead of cursing his ass out I settled for giving him a straight face. I wasn't trying to really speak since I saw the way Saint felt about him trying to push up on me. Not that there was anything going on with me and Saint, but that shit didn't matter when it came to loyalty and respect. I would forever love and respect his ass, even if he pissed me the fuck off most of the time.

"Say love, I keep seeing your fine ass 'round. You need to fuck with a real nigga, let me get your number." He said looking me up and down.

Yup just like a typical ass nigga. Only thinking about one damn thing and that shit wasn't going anywhere. I couldn't stand that big headed fake shit either. If he was so damn real he wouldn't have to say shit.

He was a fraud, but I decided to shut his ass down easy. I didn't need unnecessary drama since him and Saint had dealings. I didn't know how close they were, but I would just keep it moving and be polite unless he really came out his neck at me.

"I'm gonna have to pass." I said with a genuine smile. I wasn't trying to embarrass the nigga. That was the worst thing a bitch could do and I didn't want any hard feelings.

Not even five seconds later, Buck came through the door. As soon as he saw what was going on, he gave me a head nod and a cold stare to the nigga standing in front of me.

Buck always acted like a big brother to me, but he never said much. He just did crazy ass shit, like beating up niggas for messing with me or Jolie.

Buck turned his head to look behind him. My eyes followed his, to see none other than Saint walk in right after him. It was like I couldn't get away from this nigga if I wanted to.

A few days had passed since I saw him and as much as I didn't want him to affect me, I swear my pussy knew his ass was around. I gave a head nod and spoke to both of them. I couldn't let my feelings change shit between us.

"Wassup Buck, Saint." I said all nonchalant and shit.

"Was happnin". Saint said back. Of course like usual Buck didn't say shit. He was the quietest nigga alive.

"Ya'll go head and take care of that. Grab me a cold drink." He said over to where Buck was already heading off, towards the back of the store where the drinks were kept.

Whoever the nigga was that was trying to get my number, did what the fuck Saint said

and made his way up to the counter to pay
for the shit he already picked up.

It was obvious who ran shit. Now Buck was
an equal to Saint. But that other nigga must
have worked for him by the way he took
orders and walked off on command.

Saint took a couple steps in my direction
and then stopped in front of me. Our bodies
were only inches apart and even though we
were in the middle of a damn convenience
store it was like time stopped. My breathing
picked up, my heart rate sped up, and it
seemed as if we were the only two people in
the store.

"So wassup Saint?" I asked again, now
talking about why he was still standing here
in my face. I had to get myself together, I told
myself.

He leaned in and whispered in my ear
while slipping his arm around my back,
resting it there. His left his hand right on my
ass, causing chill bumps all over my body.

"I'm livin' ya heard meh. You missed me?!"
He asked in his sexy ass voice.

See it was just like his ass to be coming up
to me and sending me more damn mixed
signals. I told him before I even agreed to give
him the pussy that he had to live by the shit
he said and the agreement we made. And
that meant none of this shit.

"Whatever, nigga." I said playfully before backing up a little.

Then I patted him on his shoulder and turned myself around, walking up out the store. Acting like him touching me, being all close didn't fuck up my whole head and leave me horny as hell.

I made sure to put an extra switch in my hips, causing my ass to bounce more with each step. I could fuck around with his ass too, since he wanted to take it there. I felt his eyes watching me the whole way out.

Saint really played too damn much. He probably was just in his feelings because he saw his homeboy trying to talk to me. But I wasn't one for his games. He told me to focus on getting my life together and that was exactly what the fuck I was doing.

I got in my Benz. By the time I was pulling off, he was walking back to his car. I gave him a big ass wave and another smile showing all my teeth. Then pressed the gas and sped out of the parking lot in a fury. Yeah I loved Saint's ass but I was cool on him too.

Letting the spring breeze blow through my hair was giving me life. I was in a good ass mood and feeling really accomplished. Shit was looking up for me and Terrell and I was glad that fate had intervened and brought me back home. Back with the two other people in the world that I loved.

I headed home, or home for now. I was excited as hell to share the good news with Jolie about me going back to school. I knew her ass would hype me up.

She should be home since it was just after 3:00. Jolie loved teaching and loved kids, but when work was out, she busted ass and got the hell on. She never stayed after and did that work shit with the other teachers, as she told me since I first got back in town.

A few minutes later, I pulled into the small driveway and parked my Benz next to Jolie's Range Rover, that she had decked the fuck out. I made my way inside ready to catch up with my best friend and talk about our days.

She usually had some funny story to tell me about one of her bad ass students. Jolie was the best storyteller. Her ass got all into it and even would act shit out. There was no one like my best friend.

As soon as I stepped inside, I knew some shit was off. Jolie had all the curtains drawn and was sitting in the dark ass living room on the couch crying. She had her hands on either side of her face, leaned over with her head barely held up.

Jolie was one of the strongest people I ever knew. I only witnessed her cry a few times when we were kids and it was usually because she was mad as hell about something, not this sad shit. The crying she was doing now was the sad kind. The kind you do when your heart is broken.

I dropped my purse on the floor and headed over to sit beside her. I wrapped my arms around her and just let her cry without saying shit. After a while, she sat back a little and I helped get her hair out of her face.

Jolie was a mix of creole and who knows what else, she had an exotic look and was light as hell with beautiful natural curly hair. She kept her hair long and curly most of the time. Her face was all fucked up, blotchy red from the hard crying she was doing.

This was just out of character for her, but I was gonna be here for her no matter what had her feelings all over the place. It was the least I could do considering how she was looking out for me and Terrell after all the time apart.

"I'm sorry, I don't know why I'm sitting here crying like it's gonna make shit better." She said as she got herself back under control.

There was still a cynical edge to her voice. So I knew she wasn't alright like she was pretending to be.

"girl you know I got your back, no matter what. So tell me what nigga done fucked up and I'll handle that shit for you."

She looked at me like she was contemplating telling me. That shit surprised the hell out of me because Jolie was always an open book. She was wild, talkative, outgoing, all that shit wrapped into one. So I knew it had to be serious for her to be holding something back.

"You wouldn't believe me if I told you. You right though, his ass got me all sad and shit when I should just be saying FUCK BUCK!."

That caught me off guard. "When that shit happen?!" I asked out of surprise.

Yeah I had seen the way they looked at each other. But Buck was crazy as hell and a loyal ass friend to Saint. He was more like a brother to him than friend. I mean the nigga even lived with them for a while when we were children.

I would've never thought anything would come from the looks him and Jolie threw each other's way. But that shit was just like the same thing I was going through with her brother. So I guess I shouldn't have been that surprised.

"Honey, we been messin' around for over a year now... It ain't 'cus my brother either. He got me all the way in, and can't make up his damn mind. It's like his ass won't let me love him. He just won't commit."

I started getting mad as hell at Buck myself, based on the few details Jolie gave about their relationship. My friend was worthy of more than a hidden fling. She was a fucking catch for any nigga to have. Jolie was beautiful inside and out, had a good ass job and she was a down ass bitch all around.

Buck might have had some fucked up childhood, but he was grown as hell now and needed to have shit figured out. I didn't care that I was just now getting my life figured out with the help of others. Buck been had money and stability. He needed that emotional shit fixed.

"Damn, I'm a beat his ass. That nigga know better than having you out here like this." I said serious as hell.

My temper caused Jolie to chuckle and gave her more time to compose herself. It wasn't easy being in love with a man that didn't give the love back that you wanted and needed. Even though me and Jolie's situation were different, they were the same in a lot of ways.

I tried keeping my heart protected and stay immune to getting my feelings hurt. Jolie pushed her feelings aside for half her damn life, and now that she was trying to act on the mothafuckas, the shit was blowing up in her face. Heartache and rejection were the worst.

"He betta get his shit together, and soon too. 'Cus this weekend we gon' show the fuck out!" I kept talking, trying to help her feel better.

This weekend was Saint's Birthday. Since being back, all I heard about was this shit. Jolie was the one who planned his party and the entire damn weekend for that matter. Back when we were kids me and her always came up with some shit to surprise him with.

I remember one time us building up enough nerve to boost a watch from the mall at one of those kiosks, to give him as a present. That was right before he started hustling and bringing in real money. The look on his face was priceless but then he started asking us how we could afford it, and his ass just wouldn't let it rest.

Talking shit about how we better not be fuckin' with no bitch ass niggas and if he found out that we were, they were dead. We thought the shit was funny as hell at the time and couldn't stop cracking up laughing at his ass being all serious. We were still young and not thinking about any boys doing shit for us.

But he kept right on and wouldn't even wear the watch until we finally came clean and admitted to how we got it. But of course his retarded ass was almost just as mad if some nigga gifted us with some bread. He chased us around with his belt acting like he was gonna whoop our asses. We had to avoid him for a week afterwards.

Mentioning the party this weekend did the trick and helped get Jolie out of the funk she was in. I knew she was still hurt behind Buck's failure to commit, but the only thing that was gonna fix that shit was Buck getting his act together and bossing up like the real ass nigga he should be.

I hoped for my best friend's sake that he didn't fuck around and hurt her anymore. For his sake, he needed to handle the shit like a man be upfront with Saint. I would hate for this to come between their friendship.

But keeping secrets was foul as hell. To me, keeping secrets was the same as lying. If a mothafucka couldn't be honest than that let me know that they didn't give a fuck about the person they were lying to. You're either real or you ain't.

"Bitch, you right about that. I almost forgot..." Jolie said while standing up and moving fast as hell to her bedroom and coming back just as quickly.

She held two garment bags by the hangers in each of her hands. She handed one over to me and both of us unzipped the bags we were holding, pulling out some fire ass outfits.

Jolie hired a stylist from Atlanta to send us each an outfit for the party. She told the stylist exactly what we wanted and instructed them not to spare any expense with the shit.

"These just got here today. I almost forgot."
She all but shouted at me with the
excitement she felt.

Yeah my friend's whole mood had done a
180 and now she was getting me excited with
her ass.

Looking at my outfit, I swear, my jaw
dropped. I had never worn no shit this sexy
in real life or this expensive. I mean when I
was tried stripping, I basically had nothing
on, but in real life, my regular ass clothes
were nothing special. Most of the time I
bought them from the clearance racks at
Walmart. The only designer shit around me,
was what I could get on sale and keep Terrell
laced with.

I held the dress up admiring it. My outfit
was an YVES Saint Laurent black sequined
strapless mini dress. It was a stretchy
material, and from how little it was I knew
that it would cling to all my curves. I was
kind of intimidated to actually wear
something so damn expensive and sexy. It
was paired with the new Rihanna Manolo
strappy heels.

After looking over the dress, I turned to see
what Jolie's outfit looked like. Her shit was
just as nice as mine. It was a Versace mini
dress with cutouts on each side in the waist
area. There was a pair of black and gold
embroidered boots to go with it.

This bitch even copped jewelry to match, diamonds and all. My girl was not fucking around with getting us right for this weekend's celebration. There wasn't a doubt in my mind that we would be on a whole other level than the other women in the city.

Not that we were in competition with anyone, but damn these outfits were just that fly. I didn't even need to try mine on to know it was gonna look good as hell.

"Damn these some straight fire." I spoke up being all giddy and shit, almost jumping up and down.

I really didn't go out much. I went to the club with one of my exes a few times and once with Jaquan for a few hours. It always seemed like too much effort for no reason. I never got a chance to enjoy myself like other girls who were around friends, who were free of the stress that constantly plagued my mind.

Every time I did anything outside of working it felt wrong. I didn't have enough money to blow going out when bills needed to be paid, and best believe I never let a nigga pay for shit. That way they never felt like I owed them a damn thing in return.

Now this weekend I was gonna be turning the fuck up with my damn sister and celebrating Saint. He deserved that shit too. He really was a boss in every sense. He took care of shit and held shit down for not only Jolie, but now me. I was grateful for his ass despite how much he annoyed me.

I only had a few hundred dollars in savings, but I already got him a gift, and couldn't wait to give it to him. Like I said he deserved this weekend.

Me and Jolie ended up trying on the dresses and then doing some housework. I was relieved to see that she wasn't letting the shit with Buck bring her down anymore.

A couple of hours later, Terrell made it home. His ass was on the phone the minute he walked in the door. That was just like his ass so I didn't even try talking to him. I would get at him later about the plans for the upcoming weekend.

He would be here in the house alone for 24 hours. It was the first time in his life that was gonna happen. Even though he was 16, I never stayed gone overnight. I wanted to go over all the rules and shit. Since tomorrow was Friday and it was the night of the party.

I cooked dinner for the three of us and me and Jolie drank a bottle of wine watching "set it off", before heading to our rooms for bed. I ran through all the details with Terrell over dinner. Jolie added a few words here and there, but her ass was a straight up pushover with him already. He could do no wrong in her eyes. He was a good ass kid, but I still stayed on his ass to keep it that way.

After turning in for the night, I laid in bed and couldn't sleep. I picked up my cell that I left charging on my bedside table since I came back home earlier. When I unlocked it I saw there was a missed call and a new message.

The missed call and text came from Saint. Seeing his name on my screen gave me butterflies even though it shouldn't. I didn't want to have those feelings for him anymore. I just didn't know how to stop them yet. I went ahead and read the message.

"Answer me" His ass was still on that shit from earlier at the store. He was playing with fire. I wasn't' even gonna respond back to him.

He really had me fucked up. I wasn't going for the booty call, friends with benefits or any of that shit. We had our one night and I wasn't dumb enough to think that my real ass feelings weren't already involved. I couldn't go there with Saint again, otherwise I knew it would lead to me getting hurt.

I would be out here just like my friend was, that I comforted earlier. All because these niggas weren't shit and didn't give a fuck about a woman's feelings. Neither one of those two knew how to love. So I would continue to stick to the original agreement, whether he liked that shit or not.

Now my body was another damn thing. I wouldn't be getting any dick again for who knows how long. And the worst part was that I knew I would never get any that even came close to what I experienced with Saint.

I fell in love with the things he did to my body. He was the only man that ever made me cum back to back. I was still sore from the way he laid it down. I would never forget the night we spent together.

I finally drifted off to sleep after thinking about everything going on in my life. I was happy as hell for the most part. The only shit that had me uneasy was Saint, but that was nothing new.

When I woke up in the morning it was the same way I fell asleep, horny as hell, thinking about Saint's fine ass and big dick.

Saint

I had been busy as hell with the takeover in Houston. I didn't have time for anything else. Me and Buck co-owned a strip club here in New Orleans, and I hadn't even stopped through to see how the bitch was running in over a month.

The club was our main spot to wash our money, so I planned to stop through later today to make sure shit was running smoothly.

That's just how shit went when you were the boss. With keeping shipments on time, staying on top of the traps and making sure my new team was on point, most of my time was taken up.

But this weekend it was my birthday and I was celebrating that shit. Me and my mothafuckin' family were gonna be lit.

On any given day, a nigga like me might not make it back home. So making it to see 27 was a big ass accomplishment. I had beat a whole lot of fucking odds with that shit.

My actual birthday was tomorrow and Jolie had put together this whole damn weekend. All I knew was the name of the restaurant we were going to for dinner tonight and that I was supposed to wear black and gold to match the colors she picked. I was cool with that since all I wore was black and the gold watches and chains I rocked anyway. I told her ass to keep shit low-key, but knowing my sister, she probably went over top with the shit.

I decided to head out early and get a fresh cut and line up. My shit had some deep ass waves and was soft as hell. That meant I had to get it cut every couple of weeks or it grew out too much. I used to keep it long back in the day and let Jolie or Nya braid the shit.

I walked into the barber shop and saw my nigga Maino was in the process of cutting some young nigga's shit and about done. I took a seat and pulled out my phone to pass the time.

The conversation between the nigga in the chair and some other clown that was waiting, caught my attention. They were talking about this new dark skin bitch they had seen around.

From the description, I knew off the bat that they were talking about Nya. What really struck a nerve and got my blood boiling was when they started going back and forth about which one of them was gonna get at her first. Like two little ass boys gossiping how bitches do.

"You know the bitch?" the one waiting asked me, when he noticed I was looking their way.

The whole shop got quiet as fuck, all conversation stopped and eyes were on this dumb ass and me. People were trying to see what I was gonna do.

I knew this nigga by name only. I didn't know him like we were cool. I didn't even fucking speak to any of the niggas in the shop besides Maino when I walked in this bitch. His ass must have been off in the head to be coming at me about anything.

Everybody in the hood knew who the fuck I was. I didn't walk around trying to prove a point to make myself seem one way or the other. But mothafuckas still knew.

I didn't say shit respond to his bitch ass. I would see both these pussy ass niggas outside and handle shit. I damn sure wasn't gonna exchange words back and forth. I didn't talk, I let these hands fly. I was a man of action, he would learn that shit soon enough. There was no fucking way I would let that disrespect of Nya slide.

I put my attention right back on my phone acting like I didn't hear shit he said. His homeboy, that was getting his haircut, tried to get him to change the subject. That nigga was smart.

He must have realized from the look I gave that I wasn't with the conversation they were having. But his friend didn't wanna let shit go. I hated when niggas tried to act hard. Real gangstas weren't about that talking shit.

He stood up and got loud, still standing by the seats across from where I was at, like he was gonna do something.

"Nigga I asked you a question. I don't give a fuck who you...." Was all he got out before I was on my feet and rocked the nigga to sleep with a punch. I followed with two kicks to the ribs. You could hear the cracking sound from those bitches breaking. Nobody in the shop said a fucking word. He was lucky to still be breathing. If we were outside, not around a room full of potential witnesses, then he would have been dead for coming at me like he just did.

I wasn't disrespectful to mothafuckas. I minded my own fucking business, but if someone wanted to come at me on some dumb shit, then they better be prepared for the consequences.

Like I thought, he was a pussy ass nigga and couldn't even take a hit. His friend was literally on the floor trying to get his ass to wake up, while I stepped over him like he wasn't shit and went to sit down in Maino's chair, that the boy just stood up from.

"Get yo' boy outa here, and stay the fuck away from shawty..., ya heard meh!" I said looking at the nigga trying to help the other one out.

At least he wasn't trying to act like he was about that life. I saw the fear in his eyes when I said that shit. I didn't have a doubt in my mind that he got the fucking message and would relay that shit to his partna. No niggas from around this way were gonna be with Nya.

I shut that shit down right here in this shop today. Now everyone knew that she was connected to me, and that was the way I wanted it. She didn't need any distractions getting in the way of the shit she had going on.

Her ass thought I was staying away, and that shit was true, but I still knew exactly what the fuck she was up to while I had been away. I dropped her Benz off and made sure it had a GPS tracker in it. I wasn't taking no chances with her or my sister.

I didn't do all that security shit like a lot of niggas that were in similar positions as me. Even the other bosses in New Orleans had a team of niggas around them at all times. So far I hadn't needed shit like that. Me and Buck were able to look out for Jolie and I didn't give a fuck about anybody else.

Now that I was moving out to Houston for the next few months, I had to figure some shit out with security.

"Damn nigga you serious 'bout a bitch! I never thought I'd see the day" Maino said once both them niggas were out of the shop.

Most mothafucka's wouldn't dare speaking to me on some personal shit. But me and Maino was boys back in grade school coming up. So I didn't mind the shit. I still wasn't gonna sit around like a bitch and gossip and shit, but I was letting it be known that she was off limits.

"You remember Nya." I said, and that was all it took.

"Damn she back." He said and that was it. The conversation was over and Maino ended up hooking me up.

After leaving the shop, I wanted to unwind and get ready for tonight. I hopped in my ride and headed over to the strip club. I figured Tameka's ass would be there and right now I wanted to fuck. She stayed ready to take care of me.

I hadn't gotten any pussy since fucking with Nya and tonight I would be around her ass all night. Temptation was a mothafucka and I didn't want to fuck up, when we both agreed that shit wasn't gonna happen no more. I already fucked up with asking her if she missed me. I don't know where that shit came from, but I needed to get it together.

Tameka was dark skinned and built like Nya. She kept her hair short and her face was average, nothing special. But she could ride the dick and make me cum off her head game.

After parking my car, I headed inside the club. I made my way over to my office in the back once I was inside. Before I got to the door to my office and was able to unlock it, Tameka happened to walk out of the dressing room in the back.

She came up on the side of me leaning her back against the wall.

"Hey baby, when can I give you some attention?" Asking when I was gonna bless her with some dick.

I reached my hand over and cupped her pussy through the front of her pants, grabbing the mothafucka.

"Come back in an hour and I got you." I told her.

I moved my fingers rubbing on her clit, causing her to being moaning right in the hallway. I pulled my hand away and continued to go inside my office.

That way I could take care of business and do the paperwork first, then get this nut off.

Instead of just Tameka seeking me out an hour later, her and another bitch I hadn't seen before ended up knocking on my office door.

"yo". I hollered out to the door after the second knock.

I sat back in my chair, and watched these bitches walk in hand in hand. I already knew what was up. They wasted no time, stopping in front of my desk and taking off their clothes.

We only let women with banging ass bodies work in our club. Both these girls were stacked in different ways.

I got up and walked around to the front of my desk and came up to Tameka. Her titties sat up nice. She had some big ass natural breasts for how little she was and a fat ass that was fake as hell but still bounced back when I fucked her.

She eased her way down unbuckling my pants and pulling my dick out. She licked her lips and then put the tip of my dick in between her lips, sucking on it and using her tongue to circle around faster and faster.

I had never seen the other bitch before. My manager was in charge of hiring the girls and shit. She was light skin, more like my complexion and beautiful as hell. Shawty was bad all over.

While Tameka was fucking around sucking on the tip of my dick, the other hoe started rubbing on her own titties and playing in her pussy while I watched.

I didn't plan on a threesome, but I wasn't gonna turn the shit down either. I was single and these hoes were throwing the pussy at me.

The light skin girl had some smaller breasts and her body was stacked with a toned stomach and thick thighs. Her ass was big, looking like she worked out and shit. She had long ass hair that fell all over the place. She kept her eyes trained on mine and walked the few steps over to where I was standing near my desk.

Tameka was juggling my balls in her hands and started moving her mouth down my dick more. The other bitch came up behind Tameka leaning into her so that her pussy was pressed against the back of her head.

Tameka finally stopped fucking around and deep throated my shit. Even with her being a pro at giving head, she still choked on the mothafucka.

I reached out and grabbed the other girl by the back of the head gripping her hair like I had wanted to do since I realized the shit was real and began kissing on her neck.

I brought her pierced nipples to my mouth with my other hand, alternating between the two, sucking and flicking my tongue back and forth. Her nipples got hard as hell and I pinched them, making this bitch come up on her tiptoes and moan.

She was still using her own hand to play in her pussy behind Tameka. Tameka kept going to work on my dick, spitting on it and then moving her mouth fast as hell, jacking it at the same time. She worked her jaws with a good ass suction, making shit nasty.

I moved my hands from the bitch in front of me breasts, down to her pussy and the mothafucka was leaking. I stuck two fingers in and her walls clamped down on them. Her shit was tight, not as tight as Nya, but tight, especially for a stripper.

I began finger fucking her to the rhythm of the sloppy ass head Tameka was giving, using my other hand to make her go faster. She started choking on my dick each time it hit the base of her throat, but her ass kept going.

I pulled my dick out of Tameka's mouth and busted on her face and on the other one's pussy at the same time. Both these hoe's pussies were fat and completely bare, the way I liked.

"Get on your knees." I said to Tameka pointing the spot in front of my desk.

I wanted her to eat the other bitch's pussy that she brought in here, while I fucked her bent over my desk. It was time to stop fucking around and get to why the fuck they came in here in the first place.

Tameka did like I said and got her ass over to the spot fast as hell.

"Eat this bitch pussy." I said as I picked the girl up and put her back down, so she was straddling Tameka's face with her legs spread wide. I had her ass turned around with her back facing me, and her pussy sitting on Tameka's face. Her ass was tooted up in front of me.

She put her hands down on the desk for support while leaning all the way forward on it. Tameka began sucking and finger fucking her like I told her to. Lil' baby was getting into the shit. She began riding Tameka's face hard as hell, grinding down on her tongue. Popping her pussy making her ass bounce up and down.

I came up behind her and ran my thumb down her ass crack before sticking a finger in her pussy. Tameka kept sucking on her clit, driving the bitch wild.

"Yes, yes" She moaned while I gripped her ass helping her move faster over Tameka's mouth. Her body tensed up and I felt her cum on my hand.

After that her body relaxed and she acted like she was done from just cumming off a bitch eating her pussy. She had no fucking idea what she was in for.

My dick was hard as hell again ready to fuck. I leaned down and got a condom out of the wallet in my pants, and rolled it down on my shit. Wasn't no way I was gonna feel the pussy raw no matter how tight she felt. She was still a stripper and a hoe that came in here to fuck. I didn't even know shawty's name. That said all I needed to know. She came at me like a hoe, so I was gonna treat her like one.

I pushed her head down onto my desk and applied pressure to the back of her neck to keep her that way. Her fat ass was up in the air and her back arched. I lifted her ass up some more so her pussy was at the right height and then let all 10 inches slide in, in one stroke.

"FUCK Kwame!" The bitch screamed out.

I was caught off guard for a minute with her using my government and shit and paused altogether, with my dick buried deep inside her.

Nobody called me by my name outside of Jolie when she was mad as hell or Nya back in the day.

That shit rubbed me the wrong way and almost made me pull out the bitch and send her on her way. Instead, I slapped the bitch on the ass and gripped both of her hips hard as fuck, before sinking my dick even deeper in throwing that shit in her ribs.

I didn't know how the hoe knew my name or why she felt comfortable using the shit like she knew me like that, but I was just gonna get this last nut off and then get the hell out of here. Some shit was off with the bitch, and now the way her and Tameka came up in here was suspicious as hell to me.

I had all but forgotten Tameka was eating the bitch's pussy too until she reached her hands around the girls thighs and started rubbing on my legs while I was beating her shit up. I wasn't letting up either.

She was screaming and trying to run from the dick, but shit she wanted it.

Usually I would tell the girl to stay still, but I wasn't about to say shit to this one. She was here on some other shit, so all she was gonna get was the dick, not a single fucking word. I moved my hands down to her thighs and pulled her back into me more. She couldn't take the dick, but I kept digging in her guts anyway. Her body began shaking, while I kept doing all the work to get my nut.

I held her and began rocking her back and forth. Her titties rubbed against my desk hard, causing a squeaking noise with each hard stroke I laid on her. Her walls clamped down around my dick and her whole body tensed the fuck up.

I pulled out and tore off the condom while I jacked my dick a few times, busting on her ass and back letting it drip down her crack. I usually laid pipe on these bitches and took my time, but with this hoe I wanted to hurry the fuck up and bust.

I was tired of fucking with shady ass bitches. First Martina and now this one coming at me on some bullshit when all I wanted was to fuck. This shit was too much of a damn headache for what it was worth.

Tameka pulled herself back and got up. She turned around and leaned over the desk right next to the where the other girl was still trying to recover, ready for me to fuck her next.

I slapped her on the ass and then went over to my clothes on the floor, to put my pants back on.

"Naw baby, next time. " I told her.

She turned around ready to object and say some shit, but she knew I was the boss. I didn't ask her for the pussy. She came in here ready to fuck and brought this other hoe with her.

I wasn't in the mood to fuck with either of them now. When the one I fucked, used my name, that was it for me. I went off my gut and my gut was telling me these two were on some other shit.

Both of them went ahead and got dressed and left my office without saying anything else. I didn't even pay their asses any mind when they tried more than once to get my attention by bending over all extra and shit. I never chased pussy. I didn't fuck with hoes that came with extra shit or baggage.

I wouldn't be fucking with Tameka or her home girl again after this shit. Pussy was pussy and the next bitch was the same as the last.

I started thinking about Nya as I finished getting dressed. I couldn't help comparing the shit we did to what I just did with these two. I didn't have to worry about ulterior motives and with her. When we fucked it was real.

I loved her and would gladly lay down my life for her. I respected her. Shit, I even had her name tatted on me.

I knew she saw that shit too. I wished I could be that nigga for her, but I doubted that shit was possible. Me fucking random bitches, threesomes, shit like this, was all I knew. That love and relationship shit was against everything I believed in.

Thinking about her did make me feel like shit. Knowing that I was out here fucking around, when it should have been her I was with. Knowing that if I really wanted, I could have her ass on lock anytime. I was the one that kept us from being more. I didn't have any reason to feel guilty since we technically weren't together, but damn shawty had my head and heart all fucked up.

I went over to the bar in the corner of my office, opened up the bottle of cognac and threw back two shots before heading back out. I needed to get back home, shower and get ready for the night. I was looking forward to celebrating and couldn't even lie, I wanted to see Nya and be around her ass again.

Hopefully fucking this bitch ahead of time would be enough to keep me focused and my hands to myself.

Jolie

Me and Nya checked into the Ritz Carlton early so we could get ready here instead of at my house. We had four rooms checked out for two nights, but I wasn't planning on spending any nights alone that was for damn sure.

One of the rooms wouldn't be used at all, but my brother didn't know about me and Buck yet so we were gonna have to keep it on the low. I was so past this hiding and pretending with Buck that it wasn't even funny. I hated being dishonest with my brother, so he needed to get his act together quick.

Even though the birthday celebration was happening in our hometown, I wanted to make shit as big as possible. We could have easily just stayed home, but I wanted to do it big for my brother's birthday.

As he got deeper into the street life, he at least let me start throwing parties for him. Which was way more than he used to.

Most men in his position would be living a whole different type of lifestyle because they could afford it. That wasn't my brother though. He was humble and didn't want to draw attention to himself.

That didn't mean he didn't draw attention on his own, whether he tried to shine or not.

Some people just were born leaders and he was one of them.

His stubborn ass was the reason why I stayed my ass in school, had food to eat when we were kids, and was now a teacher. He always looked out for me. This get together tonight was the least I could do for him.

Every chance I got, I did the most for my brother. That's why I was glad he never took these hoes serious either, because I knew I would have had to fuck some of them up.

I wanted him to get his mind right and take a shot with Nya. I thought with her staying over the other night, that they would have figured shit out. They were meant for each other. But it didn't seem like he was ready for all that.

I knew my brother had trust issues and he had a fucked up view on love and shit because of our pops and his mother. But he should be able to easily love my girl. He had known her long enough and whether he admitted that shit or not, he was already in love with her.

Niggas were something else though. Since breaking down and crying my eyes out yesterday, I had somewhat gotten myself together. Me and Buck had a long ass conversation this morning. He made it seem like he was ready to make shit work for real, or at least try. So after this weekend he was supposed to come clean to Saint and let him know what was up.

Buck was probably the only nigga who wasn't intimidated by Saint. That was one of the many reasons why I felt like we could really work. Not to mention our bond was strong as hell and we brought out the best in each other.

I asked him straight up if he was gonna ask my brother if he was cool with us being together. And of course my man laughed and said, "if I say some shit, Saint gonna respect it, that ain't nothing."

It was easier for me to believe he was keeping us a secret because he didn't want to fuck up him and Saint's friendship. But the simple truth was, he didn't want to be in a relationship with me and fully commit. That shit hurt me to the core. So if he didn't man up and claim me after this weekend I was done. For real this time.

There were still some things that Buck didn't want to tell me and I didn't push the issue. I knew from Saint that he had a fucked up childhood, but neither one of them said shit else about it.

All I knew is one day Buck went from being over a lot to living with us. Our granddaddy didn't say shit because by that time Saint was already hustling and providing for us. Our granddaddy was cool with whatever we did as long as it didn't interfere with him or cost his ass money.

Saint started throwing more paper his way and that took care of any shit he might have talked about Buck living there.

If I had my way, tonight me and Buck would share a room. That's what I planned to happen anyway. After he saw me in what I was wearing, his ass wouldn't be able to stay off me.

When it came to us making love, or fucking, whatever it was... we did that shit like some porn stars. Without all the drama and shit that came afterwards from me wanting more. The chemistry between us was off the damn chain. Just thinking about my man got me excited to see his ass and horny as hell.

I walked out of the on-suite bathroom that connected to the bedroom, making my way over to the big ass bed. I sat down and buckled the new boots that finished my outfit.

There was a knock on my door. I figured it was Nya since I told her to head over to my room when she was done getting dressed in hers. I was gonna curl her hair and style it. She wasn't one for wearing weaves or doing hair. She confessed that while being away she had only worn extensions a handful of times.

Nya was beautiful no matter what her hair looked like, but tonight I wanted to make her feel like the queen she was. Plus, I couldn't wait to see the look on my brother's face when he saw her.

I already styled my own hair into a high bun on the top of my head. It went with the sophisticated sexy look of the dress I was wearing. I was gonna keep Nya's in a side part with loose curls. Tonight we were both gonna turn heads and I was excited as hell for my bestie. She hadn't even gotten to do no shit like this before, so I wanted to really show her how good life could be.

We both needed to look to better days and live it the fuck up.

Me and Nya were like night and day when we stood next to each other. She had a beautiful dark complexion with defined cheeks, full lips and a toned slim thick body. I often wished my body was built like hers.

I got plenty of compliments on my physique. I was short, standing only 5'3". My waist was snatched, but I was thick as hell throughout my ass and hips. There was no thigh gap for me, and my breasts were too damn big in my opinion. They were Double D's and still spilled out of most of my bras.

Now all the men loved my look, but I really would have been cool with having half the amount of breasts and ass that I did. The shit got in the way most the time. I was also self-conscious about being so light skinned. Bitches hated me for that shit from the time I was a little girl. Even to this day women threw shade on a daily basis.

Nya never made me feel like anything was wrong with me and I loved her for that. She always boosted my ego and tried to reassure me that bitches were just envious because their niggas would rather have me than their ugly asses.

She got just as much shit for being dark skinned. What I came to realize was that bitches were so insecure about themselves, that they wanted every other woman to feel how they felt.

It was tough as hell for me coming up and having a body and look that stood out from everyone around me. Bitches also tried to be funny because me and Kwame didn't look anything alike, since we had different mamas.

One time some girl he was fucking talked shit in front of him, about how I couldn't be his sister. His crazy ass came home and told me about what happened. He got me and Nya and we rode around until he found the girls brother later that day and beat his ass for that shit in the middle of the street. He left him leaking and laying on the pavement with a busted head, and probably a broken nose at least.

Then he took me and Nya over to where the girl lived and had us beat her ass too. I remember him telling us to never let anyone get away with thinking they could disrespect either of us, otherwise mothafuckas would do that shit all the time.

I found out later that when the girl said that shit in front of Saint, he made her jump out of his car while he was driving with a gun to her head. My brother didn't play any games when it came to his baby sister.

After he did all that, I didn't hear what people said anymore. But I knew what people were still thinking. I even caught shit from my granddaddy about how I supposedly acted different because I was "light skin".

That was how me and Buck started getting closer too. One day he caught me all down and shit trying to cover up the tears some dumb hoe and my high school sweet heart caused.

I was with Kenny for two years in high school. I kept the relationship a secret from my brother so he didn't end up killing the nigga. But that shit blew up in my face because Kenny used me keeping us on the low to his advantage and started fucking with this girl I had been hanging with after Nya left.

The two of them almost broke my spirit when I walked in on them fucking. I lost my mind behind that shit and snapped on their asses. I started whooping the hoe's ass and then turned on Kenny.

After I landed a couple of punches and slapped him too many times to count, he finally spoke up and the shit he said just added to my self-doubt and pain.

I remember it like it was yesterday when he shouted at me, "Damn just take yo' ugly ass on, don't nobody want your funny looking ass. Get the fuck out of my shit."

I was shocked by how Kenny was talking to me and the shit he said left me feeling like something was wrong with me. He might have been dogging me out the whole time and only fucked with me for who my brother was, I didn't know. But the shit made me feel like no matter what, I would never be good enough.

Now that I was older and knew more shit about the world, I realized that he was just mad because I was giving his bitch ass the business in front of his hoe. The way I was handling him and laying hands on him without him even being able to stand up and be a man to hold me back showed how much of a bitch he really was.

Then when I got back home, nobody was there except Buck. Usually it was like he tried to avoid being alone with me. Especially during my high school days. He stayed around my brother almost all the time and never was at the house without him.

He passed me in the hallway while I was going back to my room, ready to let my tears pour out from the pain I felt after having my heart broken.

He looked over at me and saw the tears and that was it. He grabbed my arm and stopped me from walking any more. He said some shit that sent chills through my body and were just as memorable as the hateful shit Kenny said.

"No nigga's worth your tears shawty. You better then all them." He said that shit with sincere eyes and a voice that was so deep and filled with emotion.

Buck never showed emotion or spoke on shit. I mean he could be around people and not say two words the whole time. So the fact that he did say anything meant the world to me. He meant the world to me and his opinion of me was everything.

Nya's ass started knocking again, this time louder with her impatient ass. I stood up and walked over to the door ready to help my best friend get her hair right.

I needed to get my thoughts back on the night and focus on my brother anyway. I had been spending too much time this past week thinking about Buck and what a relationship with him could be like. I was tired of thinking about his ass even if I loved him.

Instead of Nya being at the door, it was Buck that came into view as I opened it wide thinking it was my girl.

Since he said that we were really gonna do this thing and try being a real ass couple I was happy as hell to see his ass. Which was a change from how I was yesterday. It was up and down with this man.

I looked up at his fine ass, standing at my door and smiled wide enough that I'm sure my dimples were even showing.

"Damn it's good to see you're happy to see your nigga." He said as he walked in the room behind me.

I walked back over to the bed to pick up the jewelry. Since he was here I was gonna have him help me fasten the diamond necklace that the stylist sent over for me to wear with the outfit.

I picked up the necklace and then walked a few steps over to where Buck was standing. He looked like money too, wearing a Tom Ford suit that made him look even better, if that was possible.

I was impressed that his ass listened to me and wore a suit after all. Him and my brother were street niggas and usually wore jeans

214

and T's and shit. Tonight we were going to a nice ass restaurant before heading out the club. We would be up in VIP section at the club, but we were gonna be fly as fuck in there.

After the club closed I planned to finish the night off right by going over to the strip club they owned, and having a good ass time.

I hoped that there wasn't any problems on Buck's end that popped up this weekend and stopeed him from celebrating with the rest of us. The only problem that ever came up, was his baby mama from hell.

Buck was all fucked up by his past, but had managed to slip up and fuck a hoe that he had a baby by. And yes she was the definition of a hoe ass baby mama. The ratchet kind that did nothing but bring drama wherever she went.

I wasn't gonna let her get between us though. They never were in a relationship or nothing to begin with. She just happened to get pregnant and luck the fuck up because Buck was a paid nigga. She didn't know we were together yet, but I expected her to try some shit the moment she found out.

I held the necklace out and turned around while pulling up my hair in my hands to keep out of the way while Buck snapped the clasp.

"What you want me to do with this?" He asked like he really didn't know.

His ass probably never did no shit like this before though, so I told him,

"Just put it around my neck and clasp it, Please...." I said in a pleading voice all playful with him.

He did what I told him and I felt the necklace to make sure it was secure and straight.

I turned back around and of course this nigga was ready to fuck. He started to feel on my booty from behind right after he put the necklace on me.

Now that I was turned back around and still close as hell to his body, all that did was make him more aggressive. I wasn't planning on messing with him until later, but he was my weakness and I couldn't say not to him.

He gripped my thighs from the front and then brought my dress up over my ass so that my black thong was exposed and the see through part in the front was visible.

He looked down then moved his hand and patted my pussy through the fabric. That shit felt good as hell and my whole body was on fire wanting him to touch me more.

I lifted up my leg and placed it on the side of the bed while I began to work the thong down fast as hell. Nya was still supposed to be here any minute so we were gonna have to make this quick.

"Why you rushing?" He asked as he pulled me close while we were still standing up. He had taken off his pants and was completely naked. I still had my dress and boots on but Buck always liked to have sex completely naked, so no clothes got in the way and shit.

I didn't mind looking at his sexy chocolate complexion, six pack and broad shoulders. I was only half his size but I always felt on as much of his body as I could. It was rock solid all over not to mention I was in love with this man's dick.

The time we spent together left me feeling like he was all mine, but so far it was only behind closed doors. I was ready to be able to really be claimed by him.

"Nya spose to be here in a minute." I said. Turning around and tooting my ass up while I hiked my dress up even more.

"I don't give a fuck. This my pussy right?" He asked bossing the fuck up on my ass.

Buck put my ass in check real quick. He said I always tried to act like a teacher with him and tell him what the fuck to do. So of course he did the exact opposite of whatever I said. I should have known better because now he was gonna make sure to take his time and fuck me slow. But that shit didn't sound bad either. Nya would understand.

I didn't say shit back but just backed my fat ass up so that the head of his dick was pressed up lightly against my pussy.

He really was fucking around with my ass because he slowly eased his big ass dick in me inch by inch, letting my walls swallow him up.

He was stretching me as wide as my pussy could go. It gripped his dick tight as fuck, especially because he was taking his time working it in.

When he was as far in as possible he rocked his hips and moved in a circular motion hitting every damn spot I had. That shit caused me to scream out. I wanted to run and take more of him.

My mind and body was all fucked up. I tensed up to where it was hard for him to move and then started popping my ass letting the rhythm of his strokes be in control, until I exploded. My juices instantly freed up his dick and movements.

Before I could even recover from cumming, he started fucking the shit out of me trying to kill my shit. Buck always had a bipolar ass personality. One minute he was loving on me and then he would beat it up like he hated my ass. Either way his dick drove me wild.

I reached around and gripped one of my ass cheeks so he could get a full view. He slapped my ass hard digging deeper than I thought possible. I let go and went down on my elbows making and even deeper arch while he began stroking me slower and slower.

I was gonna make his ass tap out first and give me what I wanted. I started really making my ass bounce more with every movement he made. Since he had me locked down and I couldn't twerk on his dick the way I wanted.

He gripped the top of my ass and pushed into it. I was in so much pain from the way he was fucking me, I couldn't even move an inch. He had my ass locked down.

I knew he was getting closer to cumming from how his dick pulsed, but before he did, he flipped me around.

Buck took the time to lift my legs and throw them over one of his shoulders while bringing my ass in the air at an angle. Both my legs were squeezed together and his dick wouldn't fit right so I moved my hand down and grabbed the shit.

I held onto it and worked him into my pussy. My juices were soaking the bed and my hand by the time he was inside of me again. He went at a nice steady pace. His dick rubbed my clit from the inside making me cum back to back.

"You tryin' to make me cum?" He asked but he already knew that I was trying to go for a quickie. He was playing around right now and he knew I couldn't really talk while his dick was inside me. It was too much and too big to think about shit else besides the feelings he caused.

So I nodded my head.

"You want me to cum?" He asked again and he locked eyes with me.

I began grinding on his dick, trying to take more and more of him. I wanted every fucking inch in me.

"Mmmhhhm, cum baby" I said. That shit drove him crazy when I talked to him during sex. He gave me a few more strokes and my body began shaking again as I cummed all over again.

He leaned all the way over locking me in place and dug deeper than I thought possible. As soon as I felt his body get tense, I knew I fucked up.

I wanted him to cum, but damn not inside me. I wasn't ready for no baby with Buck. Maybe one day when we were married and shit, but not now not like this when were finally gonna be a couple to the world.

I hurried up and pushed him up off me and rushed to bathroom. I sat on the toilet and tried to get all his cum out of me. Then I went ahead and washed with a rag and some body wash in the sink.

I wasn't mad. It was just as much my fault as his, so I didn't have a right to be upset about the shit. I wasn't trying to have a baby yet though.

Buck was a good father and I loved his ass probably too much, but I wanted a child only when I had stability to offer with both a mother and father. Since I didn't have that shit growing up, it was important to me. I was gonna be married before I brought a child into the world.

Buck noticed my fucked up mood and came up behind me in the bathroom. Damn we looked good as hell together. He wrapped his arms around me and kissed me on my neck.

We knew each other like we had been together for ever. So he knew how I felt about kids. I was glad that I didn't have to explain the reason for how I was acting.

He didn't say anything about it and we just stood there for a minute while I got my hair laid back down. There was a knock at the door and I was thankful for the distraction. Sometimes shit got too real between me and Buck.

I guess he wasn't the only one dealing with shit from his past. I hurried up and put distance between us and made my way over to the door. It was time to get back focused on the night and the good ass time we were about to have.

Nya

As soon as my girl opened the door to her room and I saw Buck sitting in one of the lounge chairs smoking a blunt I knew what her hoe ass had been up to.

I started smiling a knowing smile as I walked in the room after her. When she turned around she had a smile on her face too.

Yeah there was nothing like some good ass dick to put you in the right mood. I couldn't even be mad, shit I wish I had some of whatever she was getting that had her happy as hell. But that wasn't happening any time soon, if ever again.

All day I had been thinking about Saint and the night we spent together. It didn't help that the anticipation of seeing him and being close to him all night was consuming me.

Jolie went into the bathroom and acted like nothing was out of the ordinary even though I just passed by Buck. His ass was sitting there looking real relaxed.

"You ain't gotta say shit 'bout that nigga sitting in your room then!" I said loud, making sure his ass heard me too.

Yes I was definitely gonna clown both their asses. Then she looked at me with that same big ass smile showing teeth and dimples, and started popping her ass.

223

We both busted out laughing and. I gave my best friend a high five. Her ass didn't fill me in on all the details because Buck was in the other room.

But all I knew was whatever agreement or make up they were doing was better than the shit the other day. I didn't wanna see my girl out here a fool behind any nigga, feeling down and out. She was way too beautiful and smart. She was a real bitch and a catch for any nigga.

No matter if Buck was like a brother to me, he better really have his shit together now.

Jolie took her time flat ironing my hair. She used the best products and by the time she was finished my 22 inches were looking perfect.

I didn't really know how to take care of the shit. She was on my ass every day about it too. I just tied it up in a ponytail or bun almost every day. She ended up styling it into loose curls and giving me a side part with a sexy side swept bang.

I was loving the way my hair looked with the dress I had on. The strapless dress fit my body and gave my waist even more definition than usual. My body was a natural hourglass figure but this dress brought out all my assets. Even my cleavage was sitting up right just like my ass that almost came out the bottom of the dress. Thankfully there was a band at the bottom hem that cuffed my ass and kept it down just past it so I wouldn't have to pull it down all night. There was a big ass difference between cheap shit and this designer dress I had on.

My girl looked laced the fuck out too in her Gucci shit. We were killing it. As we both stepped out of the bathroom, it was obvious that Buck was thinking the same thing I was about Jolie. I saw the love in his eyes and the desire too. That nigga for sure loved her ass.

While they were booed up talking, I went over to the full size bar that was in each of the hotel suites and poured me and Jolie a double shot of patron. Buck already was sipping on some shit.

We went ahead and downed the drinks and then headed out down to the lobby. Saint was supposed to be downstairs with a couple of other niggas on their team. That was what Jolie had told me, otherwise I wouldn't really know shit about what was what or who was who.

It turned out one of the two other men standing in the lobby with Saint, was the same man that had been trying to holla the last few times he saw me. I understood why Saint took that shit so personally. Even though he had made it clear that I was off limits his homeboy still was standing here eye fucking me as I came up.

225

Saint must have caught that shit too because he cut his eyes at him, which caused the nigga to change his face real quick.

When Saint looked back at me, he was watching me like a damn hawk too. But that shit gave me butterflies and brought those feelings I was trying to forget right the fuck back that quick. There was nothing like the looks that Kwame Harris gave me.

Every time he looked me up and down chills ran through my body. Now that our bodies knew each other intimately that shit was ten times stronger.

He looked good as hell too and I was gonna have a hard ass time sticking to our agreement and keeping things on the friend basis like we agreed to. But I was determined to try.

We headed out, even though it was just the two of us girls with a team of niggas. That shit didn't matter since we were always up under Saint and Buck back in the day. It felt normal. There were two other girls that met us at the restaurant. I was cool either way. I wasn't trying to fuck any of these niggas tonight anyway.

I learned that the man who had been trying to push up on me, name was Smoke and the other one's name was Drew. Drew was a nice looking white dude that had it going on.

All of us fit around one big ass table at Galatoires. Galatoires was probably the best restaurant in New Orleans. It was some real fancy shit. Being here made me appreciate how much my life switched up over the course of a few weeks.

I went from the bottom of the barrel. Being on stage about to take my clothes off to make ends meet. Now I didn't even have to work. I was living the best damn life now, out to eat wearing designer clothes eating expensive ass food.

The realization was almost too much for me. I got caught up in my head and thoughts and barely touched the food on my plate. I had ordered the Chicken Creole.

All through dinner we were drinking and having a good ass time. Saint sat at the head of the table like a damn king. I was two seats down sitting beside Jolie.

I was grateful to be here apart of this celebration for the man I loved, with the people I loved. But the thought of this all being taken away or my life going through some more bad shit kept creeping up on me.

Saint must have noticed my mood changed and he got up to switch seats with Jolie. I was embarrassed as hell because the last thing I wanted to do was fuck up his night.

So I put a smile on my face and tried acting like shit was cool. Saint wasn't having it though. His ass picked up my fork and I swear on everything his ass knew me almost too damn well. He knew exactly the right shit to say and do.

He started trying to feed me bite by bite. I know mothafucka's around us were looking at us like what the hell was going on. At first I wasn't gonna open my mouth but when he put his thumb on my bottom lip, I did like he told me.

His touch could make me do whatever the fuck he wanted no matter where the hell we were. It was like we were the only two here, the same way it always was when I was around him.

"Open your mouth." I did like he said without hesitation. "Wider." He said looking me intensely in the eyes.

There was so much sexual tension between us. His voice turned me on and him telling me what to do only added to that shit.

No more words were spoken. I let him feed me three bites. What started out as some simple shit turned into real sexual shit.

I was connected to him in a ways I would never be connected to another man. I laughed after he set the fork down and tried to downplay the effect that he had on me.

Saint read me like a damn book. He knew when I was upset and when I was faking some shit. But thankfully he let shit slide and distracted me with holding up his glass.

He made a quick toast, and we all followed suit. Then he had ordered the table a round of shots of hennessy as our last drink before heading out to the club.

I stood up to get my belongings together and told Jolie I was gonna head over to the private restroom that was just outside the room we were eating in before we left. She was in conversation with Buck and the other nigga Smoke.

I walked out and went over to where the private bathroom was. I used the bathroom then finished up with washing my hands and readjusting my outfit.

I needed to get myself together mentally. I needed to stop thinking so negative and really let myself live. I was giving myself a mental pep talk when the door opened and Saint came in.

He didn't say shit, just leaned his back against the door while facing me. He used one of his hands to lock the door. This was the shit that I didn't want to happen and I was gonna stop things before they went too far.

Saint

I planned on keeping my distance from Nya tonight, but the way shawty looked fucked my head up. Her body was calling to me. Then at dinner I could tell some shit was on her mind.

I wanted to do whatever it took to make her feel better. I didn't give a fuck what other mothafuckas thought about the shit.

When she got up and headed to the bathroom I gave her a few minutes then made up my mind to follow behind her. It might have seemed like I was just trying to fuck, but I actually wanted to make sure she was straight. I loved the fuck out of this girl.

Having her back in my life like this was already having a big ass impact on me. I thought about her all the fucking time. The only thing kept me somewhat level headed was the takeover and running the streets.

I thought that once we fucked and I got that shit out my system it would get my mind back right. I didn't know what the fuck to do to make the thoughts stop. When she was gone it was easier to deal with since she wasn't around and I didn't have to look at her.

We agreed to keep shit on a friends basis but tonight I was gonna be more than that for her. She just didn't know it yet. I didn't want to think about what that meant. Or how things would go moving forwards. I wasn't about to be up in the club and have other niggas trying to holla at her. That shit wasn't even an option. Wasn't no way I was gonna sit back and let other niggas think she was available. Fuck that she was mine.

"What are you doing in here?" She asked all timid like she was scared or some shit.

I bet her ass was scared of being this close to me. Her pussy was mine too. Her whole fucking body and mind was mine.

I knew her pussy was ready for daddy and the thought of bending her over the sink and lifting that little ass dress up crossed my mind. I could fuck her any damn where and my dick was ready and waiting for that shit too.

But I really wasn't here on that shit right now. I wanted her to understand what I was considering was real.

"NyAsia look at me." I commanded.

She was doing everything in her power to avoid eye contact with me. Moving her gaze to the damn wall, the floor, then back up to my face.

Finally she got the courage to face me and our eyes met. She was standing a few feet away. I kept the space between us for now.

If her body came in contact with mine shit was a wrap. This woman was that fucking bad and her pussy was calling a nigga. I kept my back up against the door.

"Real shit. You with me now baby, ya heard me!" I said.

"What do you mean. We just agreed to saying friends, now you talkin' bout I'm with you. What do you want from me Kwame? I'm not even trying to fuck with you right now" She asked, with emotion all in her voice in the last part she said.

"You with me, just like I'm with you. We gonna do this thing." I said.

I had never put myself out there and I didn't know how to make her understand what the fuck I was trying to say. I was gonna try this shit, being with her in a relationship. I didn't know if it would work. But I couldn't shake the feelings and all the what if's.

The fact was that I was young, but not that young. Maybe I could settle down, maybe for her I could be the nigga she needed. I wasn't gonna change, and I couldn't be a nigga I wasn't but damn I didn't want to let her go either.

"I don't get a say?" She asked getting all bold just like the Nya I knew.

That weak and timid shit wasn't her at all. So I nodded my head and told her the next thoughts that came to mind.

"Nah, you know who I am. Fuck all that talking, when I want some of that pussy I'm a get that shit too." I said straight out still looking at her, daring her to question me.

She smiled sexy as hell, "We'll see." She thought I was playing but I meant that shit, when I wanted something I got it.

All she was doing was giving me a challenge. She would see what the fuck happened with that shit. I unlocked the door and waited for her to come over to where I was standing.

I wrapped her in my arms and reached behind her sliding my hands up under her dress. Her ass cheeks were out since she had on a thong. I gripped the fuck out of her fat ass and pulled her all the way into me.

She must have felt my dick pressed up against her stomach because she tried to back away but I held her firm in place. Then I leaned in and started sucking on her collarbone and slid her thong to the side with one of my hands, spreading her enough to start finger fucking her.

Of course her pussy was wet as fuck and she instantly starting grinding on my hand making me work my fingers harder. She leaned her head back and closed her eyes still riding my damn hand.

The shit was sexy as fuck. She didn't hold shit back like she tried to do the first time we fucked. I turned her ass out and now shawty was a certified freak. I still had a whole lot of shit to teach her. I wanted her to be the only bitch alive who could handle my dick and really know how to please me.

After she cummed all over my hand I let up. I wanted her to think about this shit for the rest of the night. She was ready to fuck and so was I but the anticipation was worth it.

I slid my out and pulled her dress back down, tugging at the bottom. She needed to cover that ass up some more. Her wet pussy, flushed face and sexy ass scent was making me rethink not giving her the dick.

I went ahead and adjusted myself until my dick was only semi-hard. She got the damn message though, I always did what the fuck I said, her ass was mine wherever and whenever I wanted.

It took Nya a few more minutes to fix her hair and get herself together. I hadn't even done shit but make her cum by fingering her. She was putty in my hands and I loved that shit. She walked out afterwards ready to rejoin the group.

I kept my arms wrapped around her waist as we approached the table where everyone was standing getting ready to leave.

There were looks from everyone, I didn't miss that shit. But I didn't give a fuck. I did what I wanted and right now I wanted to be

Nya's nigga. So that was what I was. I didn't need to explain shit to any mothafucka.

"Keep that pussy wet for me." I whispered in Nya ear.

Her body got chill bumps and I placed a kiss just below her ear.

She didn't say shit back. Probably because she was speechless. She was trying to keep herself together. The way her body responded to me wasn't new to me. Plenty of bitches did the same shit. The difference was I was just as horny and gone off her as she was me.

Tonight was gonna be some shit that nobody had ever seen before and that was me claiming a bitch. I was already prepared to keep the hoes in check and off my dick.

They were no doubt gonna be on that hating ass shit with Nya. But I bet none of them would try shit with her. And if they knew her better they wouldn't even consider that shit.

From how she handled that nigga in Houston shawty was certified and would cut a bitch quick.

The niggas should be smart enough to stay the fuck away from what was mine too. If she walked in with me that was that, and she was off limits. But I was ready for whatever whether it was my birthday or not. I never let my guard down.

We pulled up and shut shit down on sight. Our crew went straight up to VIP. I sat back and looked around. It felt good as hell to be out and cooling with my bitch on my arm and my team surrounding me.

A lot of mothafuckas showed out to show love and respect. We were deep as hell and a fucking force in the building tonight. The other crews from around the city showed up too.

I was cool with them coming to celebrate, but I also felt the tension in the air. I extended an invite to the other bosses as a show of respect. They were up in the main VIP section with me and my niggas. But they were the only mothafuckas not on my team around me. Their boys were down below.

I sat back and caught a glimpse of some bitch walking in with one of the other bosses in the city that I invited. After doing a double take at the pair walking closer to the area where we were sitting in, I realized it was the same hoe I fucked earlier at the strip club, walking with the boss from Uptown.

This shit was too much of a damn coincidence and probably a set up. So my guard went up and I moved my free hand to my hip while my other one stayed between Nya's legs gripping her thigh. I didn't want to show any change in case it didn't come to anything. Plenty of bitches were just sneaky and hopefully that was all this shit was. Nothing more and nothing less.

But that still wouldn't help if she was on some dumb shit about my dick. I just made shit official with Nya. This was the first time I ever claimed a bitch in my entire life and now this random hoe sat across from me, capable of fucking with my woman's feelings.

Even though me and Nya wasn't any kind of couple earlier, it was still a fucked up thing to do if I was really feeling her the way I was. I was more than feeling Nya I was in love with her ass. So fucking this bitch didn't even compare.

The other boss, the same nigga that the hoe was with, didn't seem to be paying any attention to the shit though. That made me think she might have some ulterior motive of her own. I was good at reading people and my instincts were telling me that it didn't have shit to do with my business.

I wasn't really feeling sitting around with a bitch that was out to get me or mine, so as soon as the new Ralo song came on I grabbed Nya's hand. Nya and my sister always used to dance around the house and shit. So I knew her ass was ready to get up and join my sister who was standing over by the balcony ledge moving to the music.

She knew better than having some nigga up in her face. I was overprotective of my sister and the niggas around here knew better that that shit.

Nya and my sister called the bottle girl over and ordered some more drinks. Me and Buck each had a bottle in our hands. Fuck it, it was my night to get fucked up. But with the other bosses and crews in attendance I wasn't about to be out of my mind. I couldn't afford to be all the way gone when there was so much shit that could go wrong, especially with Jolie and Nya here.

The two of them took their drinks and Nya came up giving me a juicy ass kiss. I grabbed her ass through the thin material of her little ass dress and then slapped the mothafucka. She liked that rough shit and I bet her pussy was still wet as fuck like it was earlier.

She walked off hand in hand with my sister down to the dance floor. I wasn't with them going off and dancing down with the big ass crowd of people. But when their asses wanted to do some shit it was hard as hell to talk them out of it. I was gonna watch both their asses close.

Buck came up and stood on the side of me. He passed me the blunt he was smoking, then spoke up.

"Happy birthday bruh."

"Preciate it fam" I said. Both our eyes were glued to the dance floor where Jolie a Nya had created a small area for themselves to dance.

I turned to my other side and it just so happened that same bitch was standing a few feet away on my other side. She was playing it off and talking to some other bitch that came with someone on her nigga's team.

This hoe was really up to some shit, I wasn't about to beef with a nigga over some hoe that wasn't shit to me. This was some heat I didn't want coming my way.

Of Couse the bitch had to speak and come at me with some stupid shit while her nigga was caught up talking to a couple of the other bitches in the section.

"It's Tonya by the way, she looked me up and down and stopped dancing altogether.

"I don't give a fuck what your name is, ya heard. Fuck outa my face." I said dismissing the hoe.

I wasn't trying to have her nigga or Nya think some shit was up. To me it wasn't nothing. Shit, I didn't even feel the pussy raw.

I turned back to look at the dance floor. As soon as I saw Nya and Jolie, I instantly was more pissed off. Buck was already on his way down to where the ladies were at. Some shit was about to go down.

I got the fuck on following behind Buck
with murder on my mind.

Nya

Me and Jolie headed down to the dance floor. I was feeling the effects of the alcohol and having a good ass time. I was celebrating my Man's birthday. Yes MY man, "Saint", Kwame Harris.

I would have never expected this shit to be true. He really surprised the fuck out of me when he came into the bathroom at the restaurant talking about we were together now.

He went from wanting to stay friends, avoiding me and then claiming me. I just hoped he didn't go back on the shit and play with my emotions anymore.

It was all hard to believe, but I decided to just go with it and see if we actually could be more than what we had always been. I would love him no matter what, whether we ended up together not.

I wasn't gonna fool myself into believing his ass was gonna stick it out. I just wasn't the type of bitch to get my hopes up anymore. But friends or lovers this nigga had my heart since day one. He should know that my love for him was a lifetime love, through thick and thin type shit. I would have to see how deep his love was for me.

There was a whole lot of people up in the VIP section, but it wasn't anywhere as crowded as the damn dance floor. It seemed like the whole city turned out for Saint's birthday.

Me and Jolie walked hand in hand so we could stay together. For the most part the people moved out our way. There were some dumb hoes that gave an extra shoulder bump. But they definitely didn't want no smoke from me or Jolie. Bitches were always hating. I never understood that shit.

Most the men knew I came with Saint since the DJ announced his entrance from the jump. But they were still looking at both me and my girl.

Shit we were laced the fuck up, stunting on these hoes. Even the bitches that called themselves doing something up in VIP weren't rocking the shit we were. Jolie pulled out all the stops. I would have been cool with getting some shit from the mall, but it did feel good for once in my life to have the best of everything, I coudlnt' even lie.

There was one bitch that really rubbed me the wrong way. I had my flaws, and I was jealous as hell when it came to Saint. I guess because I always felt like he was mine, but he never was. That was until now.

The bitch came with a whole other nigga and stayed on his arm. I knew the man she came with. His name was Ron and I remembered him from back in the day. Our parents were actually friends and our families did dinners and shit together when I was coming up.

My parents stayed to themselves and barely came out of the house other than to go to work. His family was the only friends, or acquaintances, or whatever they had.

It was strange as hell to me back in the day how my parents acted towards everybody. I always wondered why they didn't want to talk to the neighbors or go to the neighborhood cookouts. They let me go out and play and let Jolie come over, but that was about it.

I didn't know if Saint knew that me and Ron knew each other when he introduced us. I wasn't trying to speak to other niggas anyway so I didn't mention it out of respect. I would fill him in later instead of in a room full of people since the shit wasn't a big deal.

I didn't want it to seem like I was keeping secrets. I had the man I wanted so there was no reason for him to feel some way about the shit. But back in the day Ron did have a thing for me and he was actually my first kiss.

It really was a small ass world, because now it turned out he ran in the same circle as Saint. That meant he was also in the streets. From the looks of it, he was doing good for himself and was a big deal.

That wasn't the reason that hoe he brought rubbed me the wrong way. I didn't have feelings and wasn't even looking at other niggas in that way, other than Saint. The bird he brought gave me a dirty ass look before she even got a "hello" from me.

I wasn't new to the hate of other females, but the look she gave me was more than that. I could read people and she was on some other shit. I would definitely watch that bitch tonight and see what she was up to.

I was young, looking sexy and the new bitch in town. Even though I grew up here, mothafuckas didn't remember me. I was just a kid when I left and now I was a full grown woman.

Maybe I was reading shit wrong and she was just a hater like the rest. But as I looked over my shoulder up to the VIP section trying to catch a glimpse of Saint my thoughts turned to killing a bitch.

I shouldn't be so possessive but damn not two minutes after I step away a hoe is gonna step to him. This was the type of shit I would have to get used to I guess. But with the drinks and weed in my system I had a "fuck him" attitude.

I grabbed Jolie's hand and the innocent two step and bounce to the beat, dancing we were doing was all the way over for us. She started cutting up right along with my ass.

We were both rolling our hips and grinding our bodies to the music, singing along with the lyrics.

The DJ fucked up when he played the "Booty" song by Black Youngsta. The whole dance floor erupted with the ladies doing their thing.

I bent over and started popping my ass with my home girl right in front of me doing the same shit. Then I bent all the way over and touched my toes causing my ass to move even more while tooted up. I felt a nigga come up behind me.

Usually I didn't let niggas dance on me at all because then they expected some shit, just like I never accepted drinks from them either. But for a minute I just went with the shit.

I even felt the niggas dick through his pants while I grinded on him. That caused me to sober up a little bit, enough to realize that Saint was probably watching this shit.

Even if the bitch was all in his face, he didn't do shit for me to be out here showing my ass or disrespecting him like this by dancing with another nigga.

The minute I pulled away and stood up, I was already being pulled from behind. I knew exactly whose arms were wrapped around my waist. I knew his body without a doubt.

Jolie

The way Buck and my brother came up on me and sis while we were dancing was a sight to fucking see. I swear the both of them acted like the most overprotective niggas in the world.

I didn't mind though. I wanted that from Buck. It was the only way he expressed his interest in me publicly for the past two years. Tonight was no different even after the making up, but I was over the shit.

I felt like there was no point in him waiting for the weekend to be over. He should be proud to be with me and to show me off. It seemed like he kept stalling. He may not even end up doing this shit with me for real.

The liquor got to me and I was in my feelings from seeing how random bitches got to push up on my man, but I couldn't. That shit took all of my strength to deal with on the regular.

But really, me and Nya weren't trying to make our men jealous, we were just having fun and turning the fuck up. We couldn't control the niggas who stepped to us. We were some sexy ass women. Any nigga would be lucky to even be near us.

Nya did a little too much but she was just trying to have fun too. The alcohol got us both.

The way my brother and Buck reacted was overboard but I should have known that shit would happen. Both their asses came over to where we were in record time.

Saint pulled Nya back quick as hell and stood in front of her. Buck didn't go as far as pulling me back, but instead stepped in front of me.

They had the two niggas boxed in while me and my bestie could barely even see what the hell was going on. I knew both of them had their weapons on them.

We both stood back smart enough not to say shit or to try and stop what was about to happen.

"These two off limits nigga. And you know that shit" My brother spat at the one who stepped to Nya.

He didn't say shit, he just shrugged. He was trying not to look shook but his expression failed him. He realized too late that he was fucking with the wrong nigga in here.

The whole city was well aware of who my brother was. Saint was crazy as hell. He didn't give a fuck and was more ruthless than all the other bosses combined.

He didn't go out and stunt on niggas often, but when he did the stories that go back to me were hard to believe. He really didn't do more than bust heads and go toe to toe when

I was around except a few times when niggas caught bullets to legs and shit.

Maybe this nigga didn't see Nya was with Saint, but I doubted that shit too. Everybody's eyes always found the people that had the most money in the building. Most niggas and bitches were watching pockets close as hell as an instinct, paying attention to the clothes and cars and every other detail.

Thankfully, Saint didn't pull his strap and neither did Buck. I wasn't' trying to see them locked up for murder. Even though they had pull and got away with a lot of shit because of who they were and the money they had, there was some shit that would still put them away for a long ass time. Murder in a club full of people was one of them.

Saint did throw two punches to the niggas dome that caused him to stagger trying to keep his balance. Buck took a swing at the one that was dancing with me and laid the nigga out with his big strong ass.

I was caught up staring at Buck with nothing but lust, when he turned around and gave me that evil ass look he always did when some shit like this went down.

This shit was far from the first time he got at a nigga for getting too close to me when I went out. He had thrown so many punches and put niggas in their places too many times to count. This shit was getting old though.

He reached out and snatched my hand pulling me off the floor and out of the spotlight. Buck hated attention and he hated every single time he had to do some shit like this for me. But this time, I really wasn't on a mission to get him to come after me like all the other times. I was just having a good time with my girl and celebrating.

I was in my feelings about him denying our relationship publicly, but that wasn't the reason why I was showing out.

He kept the tight ass grip on my hand and continued walking all the way out to the car. We were in the club for a couple hours and would have been heading out soon to the strip club.

I wasn't surprised that we were getting ready to leave. This was when most the fights broke out and niggas ended up getting shot at the clubs. We always left earlier just in case some dumb shit popped off that didn't have nothing to do with us. My brother and Buck lived by that shit and wouldn't go out unless they left early.

They didn't mind wreaking havoc and doing any fucking thing they wanted. They could be the cause of the bullets flying but didn't wanna get caught slipping and it cost them everything over some shit that didn't need to involve them.

Buck started up the engine and then pulled out his phone texting who I assumed was my brother. What caught my attention though, was the notification. I was on that shit and saw the 20 missed calls. I was on his ass quick as hell about that shit.

"Who the fuck calling you Buck? huh" I asked back to back because his ass was acting like he didn't hear me say shit. "Who?!"

"None yo' business!" He finally raised his voice and told my ass.

That was the most emotion he gave me all night. "When you gonna stop this shit shawty? I ain't bout to be out cher' swinging on niggas foreva 'cus you in your feelings?" He said switching up the conversation.

He really hurt my feelings in the way he said the shit. It was like he thought of me as a little ass girl who was throwing a temper tantrum. Maybe I had done that some along the way, but nothing like this had happened in a long ass time.

Plus if he was serious about loving me and wanting to be with me that shit shouldn't matter. I understood he didn't want me out here disrespecting him, but that wasn't what he was worried about. If his ass was worried about that he would claim me in the first place.

I let out a big breath and folded my arms across my chest. I had a bad temper. Shit we all did. But I learned to keep my emotions in check. My job required that I not flip the fuck out on the children. I also didn't wanna lose my job by checking some of the uptight mothafuckas I worked with.

It was almost 2:30 in the morning and the plan had been to head out to the strip club to finish out the birthday celebration. I doubted that shit was gonna happen now.

I was really starting to get madder about how shit played out. The last thing I wanted to do was fuck up my brother's birthday, but it was too late now. His ass was probably handling sis the same way Buck was trying to handle me.

Probably even worse because me and Buck had been through this shit plenty of times. But Saint ain't never had to worry about a woman being up close and personal with another man. He had never cared about any of the hoes he kept around. But Nya was different. She was officially his woman now.

Buck wasn't good at holding conversations about feelings and shit, so just like I expected we drove in silence over to the hotel. Even after we got there and made our way up to the hotel suite there was nothing but silence between the two of us. The entire time we were walking and even riding in the elevator up to the top floor his ass decided to give me the silent treatment.

I mean his ass didn't talk that much anyway. But now he wasn't even trying to be close to me either. He stood on one side of the elevator and when I tried to get closer he moved away. What kind of childish shit was that?

When we got to my door I started going into MY room without him. But now he wanted to be around me apparently. His ass followed behind me after I walked in the door. I was still mad, but he stopped me after I bent over to take my heels off and picked me up sitting me down on the bed.

He took his time and got down to take them off for me. My body was his. No matter if I was mad as hell or not, I melted to this man's touch only. He had me stuck.

So just like usual he ended up forgiving me and we fucked and sucked each other for hours before finally falling asleep.

No matter how good we connected and how much I cared about his ass, some shit was gonna need to really change between us. I couldn't deal with this secret shit he was on or his half ass love. Come tomorrow some decisions were gonna have to be made.

Saint

Never in my life had I been out in public with a bitch on my arm. Then when I actually man up and decide to take a chance and try this shit out, Nya does some hoe shit.

I didn't give a fuck that she was just dancing as she kept trying to explain on our way back to the hotel. She should have never been bent over letting another nigga feel on what was mine now that we were official.

The shit was making me think that I was right along and should have never given in to my feelings for her. I never wanted to be a nigga chasing behind a woman and the way she had me feeling I would have killed both them niggas tonight.

Jolie's ass knew better too. That shit wasn't about to happen when I was around. Back when Nya wasn't my bitch, I would've still checked the nigga but the disloyalty was a whole different feeling. I never wanted to feel betrayed by my girl.

It had been the best fucking birthday I ever had. God had blessed me to see 28. In the life of a street nigga and boss like me that was a big ass accomplishment. I had been putting in work hustling for half my life. Most niggas that I came up with were either locked up, doing double digits in the pen or dead.

It only took a few minutes to make it back to the hotel and Nya was acting all upset. I'm talking bout she had tears in her eyes and all. I only seen her cry one time and that was at her parents funeral.

She was a real one and didn't show weakness much. Now she might have a bad ass temper and cut a nigga or bitch quick as hell. But this sad shit just wasn't like her. I almost felt sorry for her, but then I remembered she was the one out there like a hoe. So she needed to feel guilty behind that shit.

Before I got out the whip, she reached her hand over and placed it on my arm to get my attention. The valet was coming to park the car. I looked at her and our eyes met. It was like she was apologizing without saying a word.

I knew I wasn't gonna stay mad at her ass for long. Nya was my weakness. But her ass was gonna learn a fucking lesson.

I shook off her hold on my arm and stepped out the car handing the keys to the man that came over to the curb. I told him not to fuck up my shit. I drove my new foreign today. There was no way I was gonna let some shit get fucked up on it.

Nya took her time getting out. She finally stepped out, while I waited on the sidewalk for her. I looked her up and down and didn't see an ounce of the sad and remorseful girl that was just in the car. She covered her emotions up fast as hell. That was the type of boss ass shit I respected.

I would never put my personal shit out in public and didn't want my woman to either. Even though I didn't know none of the niggas around this area, they would know who the fuck I was. I didn't give the streets shit to talk about. They could assume whatever the fuck they wanted.

I went ahead and reached out my hand for Nya to take. She did, and we both walked hand in hand, into the hotel entrance like shit was cool.

I was definitely about to teach her ass a lesson. The more I thought about all the shit I was about to do the more my anger faded. My dick was hard as hell every time I was near Nya, especially now that I knew what that pussy felt like.

I loved everything about this woman. From her fucked up attitude, to the way her pussy tasted. So her dancing on a nigga may have pissed me the fuck off but that wasn't nothing that my dick couldn't fix. I was gonna make her remember who the fuck she was with. She must have forgot how I got down since the last time.

This would be the last fucking time she did some dumb hoe shit like that. I needed to make her understand what it was like being with a nigga like me. She might know me, but being my woman was some different shit.

As soon as I closed my hotel room door I was on a mission. I stopped her right inside the door and pushed her up against the wall. I came up close pressing my body into hers from behind and then grabbed ahold of both her hands. I lifted them up above her head and held them against the fucking wall. She was stuck in place.

Then I reached up under her dress and moved her thong to the side. I began working my fingers in and out, using my thumb to rub against her clit.

I lifted her up more and got down on one knee. I bit down on her ass cheek, and then dove face first in her pussy, working my tongue in between her pussy folds from behind. She strained against the wall, but I held her ass cheeks spread apart, keeping her lower body still and slowly circled my tongue around her entrance.

She began enjoying the shit too much, moaning and moving against my mouth. I wasn't trying to make her ass cum yet. She was gonna have to wait for that shit.

Since she wanted to play games tonight that was exactly what the fuck we were gonna do.

I pulled back away from her and stood, adjusting my dick in my pants before walking my over to the balcony door and going out on it. I left her ass standing there with her dress pulled up over her fat ass and pussy dripping wet.

As hard as it was for me not to pull my dick out and fuck her life up right there in the hall I wanted her to know who the fuck was in charge. And that shit went for everything. From fucking, our life behind closed doors to out in public. Her ass knew me well enough to know that I ran shit.

I was a real ass nigga and devoted to her. She was my world already, but she was gonna have to submit to that shit because wasn't no other way this shit would work between us.

I couldn't be out here going crazy behind shit she did. She needed to understand that something as simple as dancing with another nigga could come with a whole lot of fucking consequences for me.

I would easily murder, go to prison or do any fucking thing for her. I would lay my life down for Nya, so she had to move different and stop with bullshit like what she did earlier.

It wasn't but a few minutes before she came out on the balcony with me. She came out wearing nothing but her bra and panties.

She walked over in front of me and leaned up against the balcony ledge with her ass bent over the shit.

Her shape was sexy as hell from every view but looking at the shit right now with the moon and stars shining down giving her sexy skin a glow, made me grateful that she was mine.

She was trying to act like it wasn't nothing for her to be out here in front of a nigga like me with barely any shit on her body. She knew what she was working with.

"It's a beautiful night." She said.

I didn't say shit, I just sat back smoking my blunt and admired the view in front of me.

Nya turned around and that's when I saw what looked like a tattoo on her lower stomach above her panty line.

"Come here." I said in a harsher tone than I intended.

She stood still for a brief pause, then came over to where I was sitting. She stood above me and I was able to get a good look at her new ink. The shit was sexy as fuck and turned me on even more.

"You like it?"

I didn't answer, so she continued with what she was saying.

"It's your birthday present. You got mine, and now I got yours... I'm all yours for life nigga." She said explaining why she got my initials tattooed on her skin.

I ran my hand over them, like she first did mine when she noticed them. Then I leaned forward and kissed the letters gently. Damn I loved this girl.

Nya dropped down to her knees. Her impatient ass wanted the dick. I knew she was trying to get on my good side.

She unbuckled my pants and I let her slide them down enough that my dick came out. Her eyes got big as hell just like the first time she saw how big I was. She looked down at my dick then back up at me.

"I'm sorry." She said sounding like she meant that shit.

I nodded my head and that was all she fucking wrote. Shawty got up into a squatting position. She put her hands on my thighs and opened her mouth. Nya started humming on my dick. I'm talking about that sloppy shit too. Her spit was real nasty and she put them jaws to work sucking hard and then soft each time she went up and down.

I used my hand and held her hair back. I knew she was trying to take as much of me as she could in but everytime she deep throated my shit she began to gag. She was gonna learn to suck that shit down though.

So I lifted her ass up and flipped her around and upside down. I had her legs on either side of my head with her thighs on my shoulders and pussy close to my face.

I pulled her thong down to get them shit out the way. I positioned Nya's head just above my dick. She knew what the fuck was up and began sucking my dick again.

In this position she didn't have a choice but to take the dick. She relaxed her throat and opened wider. She began humming and vibrating the back of her throat while I started kissing her pussy lips.

To get better access to her clit I used my hand and spread her wider and then clamped down on her clit. I started sucking and flicking my tongue over the shit. Nya stopped sucking my dick altogether. Her body started shaking and she let that shit go, I kept sucking with her squirming for me to let up.

Nya tasted good as fuck, so I kept eating the fuck outa her pussy.

"Whaaat, are you doing to me?!" She let out after cumming.

I was ready to get in them guts. I lifted her back up and placed her back on her feet.

"Take that shit off. I want MY bitch ass up face down." I said and slapped her ass hard as hell.

She turned around and walked her ass right on in to the room and did just like daddy said. I followed her in.

Then stood there watching her play in her pussy from the back. She was getting into the shit, calling my name out. I came up behind her once all my clothes were off.

I slid my dick in nice and slow letting my dick stretch her walls. I knew she felt every fucking inch. But she backed up into me more. My dick hit the base of her pussy and I started laying those slow strokes on her.

"Fuck, I can't, shit!" She yelled out back to back.

"Yes the fuck you can. You mine right?" I asked while I kept deep stroking and fucking her up.

I knew she couldn't handle the way I was fucking her. I was all in her ribs and shit but she needed to remember that when she agreed to being with me that I wasn't gonna let her run all over me and do fuck shit like she did tonight.

I leaned forward and locked her ass in even more.

"Don't do no shit like that again." I said in her ear while still going in and out slow and deep as shit. "We in this shit now baby." I let her know.

She didn't say shit back. She was trying to find a way to move, but I wasn't letting up. Her body was tensed up and I knew she was about to fucking explode.

She froze up even more while her pussy squirted and tightened up about to push me out. But I held onto her shoulders and made her ride that shit out.

"Aaaahhhh, fuck. I love you!" She screamed out as she let go completely. Her body relaxed with my dick still deep in her guts.

After she was finished cumming I pulled out and turned her around. I laid down and grabbed ahold of her lips enough to lift her up and set her down on my dick. She immediately screamed out again.

Yeah she took all ten inches and sat there without moving while letting her pussy adjust. No matter how wet she was, I could tell she ain't ever had dick like what I was giving her before. She did a good ass job handing it though.

Nya smiled down at me, and planted her feet on either side of me. She began going nice and slow bouncing on the big mothafucka. I cupped her ass with both hands squeezing tight. That shit had her going wild and her body responded right away.

As tight as her pussy was that shit got even tighter. It was hard for her to move with how closed up her shit was.

"Let that shit go and ride your dick shawty. You owe me." I said while looking up at her

263

and moving my hands to her titties. I held on to them both with my hands and started pinching her nipples while she rotated her hips again going up and down and around. Handling the dick just fine.

She only grinded on me a few times before her her pussy busted. I felt that shit from the tip of my dick at the base of her pussy. She lifted up enough for me to see it. I grabbed her hips and started moving her up and down faster. Her titties were bouncing and sweat was glistened between them.

I felt my nut rising and she must have been able to tell because her ass started going harder like she was trying to make me bust faster. Her ass was trying to be in control so I flipper her over and laid another few strokes on her before we both were cumming again. I pulled out and rolled over.

"I meant that shit Nya. Your mine now, don't let that shit happen again. This for life."

She started trying to say sorry again but I wasn't trying to hear that shit.

"Nah, I said what I said, It's over now."

"I'm gonna do better, I love your ass. Always have and always will. We gonna make this shit work." She responded back, then moved closer, stretching her leg across me.

I felt like a fucking king laying with my bitch like this. Nya was the only woman who could make me feel like this. I realized that no matter what the old me, the one that vowed to never be with a bitch, was now gone.

I could never let Nya go and I would never let her bring me down either. I hoped she understood I was serious as hell when I said not to let no shit like that happen again.

Tonya

I'm that bitch that you don't wanna fuck over. I wasn't out here like these other hoes that gave away their pussy for free or without a good ass reason that benefited me.

When I came out here from Houston it was for one reason only and that was to get close to Saint's fine ass.

I had been here for a little over a month. This shit was a mission to me. When my sister first told me about the nigga she met and was fucking with I knew that I was meant to be his instead of her.

She should have never gave me all the details about how he fucked her or how much paper he had. She didn't have a clue who she was fucking with. The dumb bitch should have had enough sense to at least try and become his main. So that was on her.

I wasn't new to the game. I had been gaming niggas for years. I was only 21 but nothing surprised me anymore. Not how grimy these niggas or bitches were or how much money I could get their dumb assess to come up off of.

The way I played shit earlier and convinced one of the bitches Saint fucked with to include me in on the shit, was way too fucking easy. I even found a way to come with another boss in the city tonight to his party.

I considered giving up on the challenge of bagging Saint because he was so unattached and focused on his street shit to even approach. The nigga I was entertaining that brought me to the party had just as much clout and bread as him so I was close to just saying fuck it.

I'm glad I didn't though. Once he threw that big ass dick on me and I found out what the fuck had my sister so gone it was over with. There was no way I was giving him up now.

My sister might have been a lot of fucking things but she wasn't lying when it came to the way she described sex with the nigga.

As soon as I laid eyes on him tonight I was ready to walk over to his ass and drop the nigga I was with like I didn't come with his ass at all. Then I spotted the bitch on his arm. That shit pissed me the fuck off.

I watched his ass close as hell the whole time I was in town and he never was spotted with a bitch. The word on the street was he never gave a fuck about any of the bitches, and he kept all his shit private.

Why the hell he had this hoe on his arm was a damn mystery to me. But if what I heard about him and learned about him myself was true, this must've been some serious shit between the two. I saw the way he looked at her.

He was another sorry ass no good nigga like all the rest. That shit wasn't gonna stop me from making him mine for the time being. He was just over at my sister's place dicking her down the other day. Then had me bent over his desk earlier.

But this shit between him and the bitch on his arm looked like the real deal. I knew a nigga in love and gone behind a bitch. That was the same shit I did to niggas on purpose to trick off them.

I couldn't lie though, the bitch was fine as hell. She was stacked and even though she was on the slim side she had a fat ass and some nice sized titties on her. Most skinny bitches were built like little boys, but the hoe had a body on her.

Her body didn't even compare to her face. She was beautiful with a perfect smile and all. Seeing how happy she looked on Saint's arm did some shit to me.

The bitch was where I was supposed to be. I never came second. The jealously I felt was a new feeling to me and it only made me more determined to get this bitch's nigga. Fuck this pretty hoe and her overly happy ass. I always got what I wanted and I always played to win.

Starting tonight, I was gonna begin making more moves to get what I wanted. First, I wanted to make this nigga remember that he was just in my pussy digging in my guts a few hours ago since he wanted to act brand new. I saw my chance and took it as soon as his little girlfriend walked off with her friend.

As the two of them walked out the section her friend looked over my way and sized me up. She was some mixed bitch laced in nothing but designer shit. But the look she gave me was ice cold. I didn't even know the girl. But I didn't like other bitches anyway.

My plan was to slip Saint my phone number and room number at the hotel. I hoped he would use that shit later or when he got rid of his bitch again. But his ass got caught up behind her hoe ass. She was dancing on some nigga and Saint went chasing after the girl.

I stayed up in the VIP watching every fucking thing. He dealt with shit like a real boss. I swear seeing him pick his girl up and handle her like that being all protective and shit made me angrier that he was doing all this shit for the wrong bitch.

I should be the one he was worried about not her. My pussy was ready for another round too. Saint was too damn fine and too damn everything. I needed him to be my nigga.

Not long after all the commotion and what turned into a one sided fight, the man I came with was ready to leave. I guess tonight I would settle for the second best thing in the city. Ron was good, but he wasn't saint. Second best wasn't an option for me. I was gonna get mine, believe that.

Nya

Me and Saint were really doing this shit and had been together almost nonstop for the last few weeks. I had to admit being with him left me feeling as close to happy as I knew how to be.

Classes started the next week after I signed up since the semester just began and I didn't want to wait any longer than possible to get my GED. The sooner I got done with that, the sooner I could stand on my own and get a college education.

Each day of the week I came home from class and then got ready to see Saint. After taking our relationship beyond just that friend shit, I was learning all types of shit about him that I never knew.

Like that he expected me to touch him whenever I was around him. I mean anything from when I laid in bed with him how he wanted me to rest my arm across his chest, or even in the car he liked me to keep my hand on his arm or somewhere on his body.

I loved that my nigga wanted the attention from me and it seemed like he was really into me as much as I was him. But I was still insecure with my place in his life. I just didn't want to believe this shit was gonna last between us and then it not. I couldn't let myself get hurt.

Saint was slick as hell and always found a way to convince me to stay the night with him. I only came back to Jolie's to make sure Terrell was good and take care of him. Jolie was MIA most weekends but still came home every night.

Terrell and I ate dinner together every day and I was glad as hell that he had adjusted to life in New Orleans just fine.

Tonight was Friday and I planned ahead this time, to pack a small bag for the stay-over with Saint. I wanted to meet up with him downtown and grab something to eat.

He liked spoiling me but he tried to stay local on this side of the bridge. This time I wanted to act like a tourist since I had been gone so long. Hell, half the shit was new to me since it wasn't here when I was younger anyway.

After I changed, I walked in the living room and heard Terrell come in the house. His ass was on the phone and from the sound of it his fast ass was trying to get into some shit with whatever little girl he was talking to.

He must not have known I was home, or I'm sure he wouldn't be talking like he was. It hit me that since I had gotten to New Orleans and up and moved our whole fucking life last month, I had been selfish as hell.

I mean I knew Terrell was good and well taken care of with either me or Jolie around, but the truth was I was more like Terrell's parent. That was how our relationship was, it wasn't a normal brother and sister one.

I took care of his ass all these years and spent more years raising him than our parents did before they were killed.

I felt bad as hell for not being on his ass or really taking more time out to see what was going on with him. I needed to do better and make him more of a priority. I decided that tonight I was just gong to chill with my brother and get a raincheck with Saint.

He would be alright going without seeing me or getting any pussy for one night. That was another thing, I was completely sprung off his dick. Every time we were around each other we couldn't keep our hands to ourselves. His ass was worse than me, and I used that shit to my advantage.

I called him up and of course he was trying all types of shit to get me to come see him. I had to give it to his ass too, no matter how busy he was with all the shit he was into he took my ass everywhere with him.

The other night he took me to the movies and half way through he had to leave to take care of some shit in one of his traps. I appreciated that he kept shit a hundred and trusted me like that. But that was nothing new to us.

What was different, was that he really treated me like I was his significant other now. It still surprised me that this was my life.

I didn't care that he had to cut the night short. I knew how the street shit went. If I didn't like the shit then I didn't like a part of who he was. He was a nigga that got up and put in work. He grinded in order to stack paper.

I wasn't about to knock the way he got his money. Even when we were younger and I came from a different type of household, I always believed in that shit and believed in him.

That was probably why I was motivated to hustle and take care of my brother no matter how bad shit got for us. I knew what it meant to make something out of nothing, because I witnessed that shit first hand watching Saint hold shit down for his family.

He probably didn't know how much of an impact he had on my life. The man was everything to me that I thought he was all along.

Saint showered me with love and attention. But I knew he was still holding back some, just like I was with him. Him and Jolie both had trust issues and shit.

Jolie told me all about how he vowed to never get caught up loving a bitch and lose his mind behind her like his daddy did. He thought his pops was a weak nigga and he feared turning out the same way.

I didn't intend to do shit to fuck with his head though. I would remain loyal to this nigga for a lifetime if he let me. Even after the fallout in the club, and he called himself threatening me after we made up. He wasn't gonna be forgiving if there was a next time.

But Saint didn't put fear in my heat no matter what he said or did. I loved his ass too much and didn't give a fuck what he threatened to do. I wasn't a weak bitch and would prove him wrong anyway.

After all his attempts at getting me to come see him and me shutting that shit down over and over, he finally gave in and let me have this one time to get "my way" as he said.

Talking on the phone and hearing his voice sounding so damn sexy left my pussy on swole and throbbing. He started talking dirty to me, telling me about all the shit he was gonna do when he saw me again.

Since I didn't give in, he decided to go ahead and fly out to Houston for the weekend. That way he could finalize shit for his move and still be back to see me by Sunday night.

Saint was straight up with me when he told me that shit was about change for him.

At first, he tried to go back on making shit official with me. He said we should cool off for the time being, since he didn't want to do that long distance shit. He talked about distance and being faithful.

That shit wasn't a problem on my end. No other nigga had me worrying about dick ever. Despite Saint having that effect on me, I wasn't gonna let that impact my life decisions.

I would be straight in this life with or without him. I was with him because I really loved his ass and thought he was meant for me on some real shit.

So time, distance none of that shit mattered on my end. But I caught what he was really saying. He didn't want to be responsible for fucking up and cheating on me with a bitch. I didn't even wanna think about that because the truth was I probably would kill a bitch, now that he was my man.

I'm sure he was a hoe ass nigga before. But now that he got my hopes up and we had been rocking together, that shit ran deep for me. I expected his loyalty. Just like his ass was making threats about me dancing with another nigga. I wasn't down to share. He would find out quick too, if he thought different.

His tune changed as the time got closer for him to move to Houston for good. He was leaving Buck here and going solo into this shit. He told me about the takeover and what he was really doing out in Houston.

I wasn't trying to be involved in the street shit he had going on. I wanted to keep my life out of it as much as possible so that nothing stopped me from having a good career.

I would still do whatever needed to be done at any time though, no matter what that meant later on, if it meant protecting the people I loved. It was real shit, that he was able to come to me and trust me with whatever he was dealing with.

I wanted to be his peace but I was the type of bitch that spoke my mind even when it would be better to keep my opinions to myself.

I was okay with him leaving out for Houston. I wasn't clingy and would never try and hold my man back from reaching his potential. If he needed to handle business then he should do that shit.

It worked out too because I was trying to be a good big sister. Plus me and Jolie hadn't gotten an opportunity to catch up since we were both busy with our own shit.

I went into my bedroom and took off my Jordan's and jeans before changing into a pair of leggings. Since being back in town, my body was starting to fill out more. There was something about eating some good ass hood food.

The extra plates that Ms. Freida sent over for me and Jolie were adding to my thickness. I guess it was true what they say about a bitch getting fucked good and happy.

I was slim thick, but since I started fucking with Saint I swear my ass had gotten bigger, my thighs, everywhere was filled the fuck out.

The things that Saint did to my body was some shit that I always heard about but never believed the hype about. Some of the bitches I came across working here and there would talk about so and so's dick, how good the sex was, and how much the hoe loved giving head.

I never understood what they hell they were talking about. I swear I really thought they were exaggerating. I mean I guess it felt good when the other niggas were fucking me, but shit Saint was the truth. His ass was gone off my pussy too, so it didn't make me feel bad.

I threw my hair up and went back out into the living room. When I got back out there, Terrell came in the room a few minutes later. He was dressed like he was about to leave and go somewhere.

"Where you goin' Rell?" I had to shout at him because when I looked up he was already gone back into his room.

He reappeared a minute later with a fresh shirt on and came over to where I was sitting. He sat next to me on the couch.

"I'm 'bout to head out. I'm just gon' be on the block and with some niggas from school, aight?" He said asking if I was cool with it.

"Don't let them grades slip or your ass ain't goin' nowhere. Stay outa trouble." I said smiling at him and play punching him in the shoulder.

"I'm good sis." He agreed and then got back up to head out.

Now that Terrell was getting older I tried to keep him in check but I was young enough to know that he was gonna do what he was gonna do. I hoped he was smart enough to avoid the street shit and stay in school. I was just now getting back into it and couldn't be happier about my situation.

Since Terrell was gonna be gone most the night I went and grabbed my blanket to lay down and find some movie to watch. A relaxing night sounded good as hell to me. I hadn't even turned on this TV since the first week I was in town.

Saint was a greedy nigga and wanted all my time. It didn't matter that he was this hard ass gangsta, when it came to me it was some different shit. He was still a fucking boss, but one with a heart.

It was after 6:00 p.m. when I woke up and realized that I must have fallen asleep. I was tired as hell from all these classes and the job search.

I stood up and the house was quiet as hell. Jolie wasn't home so I checked my phone. Her ass left me a text telling me she was staying over Bucks' house. He still hadn't said shit to Saint and I was afraid this shit was gonna be a disaster when he found out.

The longer they kept it from him the worse it was gonna be. He wasn't a forgiving man and I was sure he would feel betrayed by both of them keeping this shit from him.

That was on top of Buck breaking the fucking code and fucking Jolie in the first place. Shit was all the way bad.

I fixed some leftovers and cleaned up the house some. It was still pretty early and a Friday night so I didn't want sit up here being lonely and shit.

The thought of surprising Saint in Houston came to mind and I figured his ass would be happy as hell to see me as much as he was talking shit earlier.

I called Jolie and she agreed to come back home tonight to make sure Terrell was good. Her ass sounded half asleep. As early as it was, I knew she was just wore out from Buck. They were always s fucking, similar to me and Saint.

The difference was they were on the low and Saint was ready to fuck everywhere we went. In public, all that shit it didn't matter.

I went ahead and took a quick shower after I booked a flight that left in 3 hours. The airport was only about a half hour away, so I knew I would have time.

I changed into a red bra and panty set from Victoria's Secret and threw on a sundress over it. The weather was warm enough to wear the dress with a cardigan over it. Something simple, but sexy for my man.

Thinking about Saint made me more than ready to catch the flight and touch down as soon as possible. I should make it there by midnight.

On my way to the airport I called him and played shit off too. Making the surprise that much better. He had no fucking clue what I was up to. I got him to come up off his room number at the hotel.

I told him it was just in case of an emergency or some shit went bad while he was out there. I knew I shouldn't be speaking about the serious shit he was involved in, but I figured he couldn't be mad after I surprised him.

I never was into surprises and never did no shit like this before. It was like this nigga brought out a different side to me. The side where he had my ass wide open ready to be anything I could for him.

After arriving at the airport and boarding the plane, I went ahead and leaned back in the seat as much as the little ass shit would let me and closed my eyes. I dozed off, into a light nap thinking about the same man I thought about every night.

He consumed every part of me from physical to mental.

Tonya

It was another dead ass Friday and I was out here doing fucking nothing! I mean I was at the club, but nothing was happening like I wanted it to with Saint since the one time he fucked the shit out of me in his office the first day I met him.

I was starting to get discouraged with making shit happen with him at all. He hadn't even been by the club since his birthday weekend almost a month ago.

In the meantime I continued playing shit cool with Ron and letting him spoil me. He didn't know I was still stripping. He thought I was really his bitch to be giving out orders and shit. But no nigga ever stopped me from doing shit. I loved to get money period.

This shit being at a standstill got so bad that I started fishing for information from any damn body. This past week I even went ahead and asked Ron questions here and there about the other bosses in the city trying to get any information I could about Saint without seeming like I was interested in him.

Ron didn't pillow talk like most niggas, so as soon as I mentioned anything to do with the street shit he played dumb to it all. Sooner or later I was gonna find a way to get at Saint from somebody.

I just needed to be patient and that was something I could do for Saint. He was worth the fucking wait and trouble. The work I was putting in damn sure was gonna pay off.

The opportunity fell right in my lap when Saint walked in the club before it opened for the night. I just happened to be there earlier than most of the other bitches and earlier than I had ever come to work before.

That shit was destiny. It was a fucking sign since I only picked up an extra shift in the first place because I didn't have shit else planned tonight. I wasn't even supposed to be here otherwise.

Saint saw me and ducked out quick as hell. I still caught the look in his eyes when he spotted me. The nigga liked what the fuck he saw just like every other nigga. There was no denying that shit.

He was probably staying away because of his bitch, but that shit was also about to be fixed. All the distractions needed to be handled, then he could focus on me.

That's how niggas worked. Eliminate the competition, play your role and eventually they all come around. There was a method to this shit.

I didn't have a doubt in my mind that when it was all said and done Saint was gonna be another nigga that fell victim to me. He didn't even see the shit coming.

I stayed near the bar pretending not to notice his moves and sipping on my drink. He was in and out the club in less than 15 minutes time. As soon as he was gone, I made my move.

I went over to the nigga that ran the place. I had been leading Nuck on since I started working here. He was a big sloppy ass nigga. He fucked with a lot of the bitches in the club, but I wasn't a regular ass hoe that gave up pussy without something being in it for me.

My purpose for being out here was getting a big bag and that was Saint, not this nigga.

Nuck's back was to me while he was turned around closing Saint's office door. This nigga didn't even get a real office in the club. Saint gave him a room that didn't have a door on it at the back of the hall to work out of.

That shit was funny as hell to me. Nuck seemed to be a real bitch about the shit. He never went in Saint's office without him being present that I saw. He just took the shit given to him. He was a straight bitch.

Nuck turned around. I immediately noticed how stressed he looked. I bet Saint was the cause of that shit and that would only help me get what the fuck I wanted out of his ass.

I finished walking the few steps over to where he was at, and placed my hands on his shoulders. I leaned my body up against his closing the distance between us.

My titties were pressed against his big chest. His sloppy ass stomach was big as hell, but I didn't let that shit deter me from getting as close as possible. The shit must have hung down over his dick that's just how big he was.

I guess he thought the way I was acting meant I was finally giving in and was ready to fuck. Yup I had his ass already.

He wrapped his arms about my waist and started gripping my ass. All I had on was a G-String, so he started working his hands all over my ass and hips rubbing on me.

I played it off and let him feel all over me. Shit I was over here trying to get some information from the nigga so I needed him to buy the act.

"Mmmmm, that feels so good, You look stressed. Let me take care of you daddy." I said while hugging this nigga right back.

"You finally ready for the dick?" He asked. A real nigga wouldn't have to ask for shit. I cringed but kept my act up.

"I know Saint acts like he run shit, but YOU the one who really runs shit in here. I just wanna make you feel good and ease your mind" I said gassing this niggas head full of bullshit.

"Don't worry 'bout that nigga, when you gon' let me get a sample of that?" He asked moving one of his hands that was on my ass to my pussy and cupping my shit through the G-string.

"How you gon' ask for shit and you actin' like you can't trust me." I said. "I'm trying to be that bitch for you nigga, don't play me." I laid the shit on thick trying to play up his ego.

Niggas were fools half the time and believed anything as long as it made them feel like that nigga. This man was no different.

"Word, I hear ya baby". He pulled the office key back out his pocket and held that shit up like he was really doing something.

"You wanna be my bitch, we can make shit happen right now. Saint gon' be out cher' in Houston for the night. Go 'head and Bust that shit open for a real nigga." He responded getting ready to unlock the door again.

Yup just another dumb nigga.

"Let me go finish my set then I got you," I promised.

I even reached my hand over to find his dick through his pants. I didn't want him to get suspicious about the way I came at him.

I had to admit even with how fat and sloppy this nigga was, he had a big dick. Not nearly what Saint was working with but bigger than most. That almost made me reconsider. I could ride his shit with my eyes closed and get off before taking care of business.

I wasn't pressed for dick though. I still had one crazy ass nigga around town and didn't want another. So I pulled my hand away while placing a juicy kiss on his lips, sticking my tongue down his throat and sucking on his bottom lip.

He bought every fucking thing I said and did, like the gullible ass nigga he was. He slapped me hard on my ass as I turned around pretending to head back to the dressing room to get ready to go on stage.

Once I was inside the room, I grabbed my bags, threw on some clothes and headed out the back door. I hit the unlock button on my all white mustang and opened the door.

After I turned the ignition on, I sat in the parking lot for another minute while I pulled my phone out. It was time to stop sitting back waiting and start going after what I wanted.

I found my sister's contact in my phone and hit send. My sister picked up after the second ring. Always s a thirsty bitch even when it came to answering calls from me. I would have waited until the voicemail got ready to pick up.

Everything was planned out to me. I wanted the power, money every fucking thing.

"Hey girl". I spoke into the phone keeping the real feelings I had for her out of my voice.

I mean I still loved my sister and we could be cool after I took Saint off her hands. She always got over shit when it came to me. This wouldn't be the first time I stole a nigga from her.

"What's up? When you coming home?" She asked sounding worried.

Her ass always tried to get me come home every time I was out of town making money and shit. She wasn't only a weak bitch she was lame as hell. The only reason she even fucked with a nigga like Saint was by mistake.

She never went out or was into street niggas at all. It was by chance that he crossed paths with her while she was working her shift at the bank.

He must've said all the right shit because he actually got her to let her guard down enough to give him her number.

My sister's ass was really out there with him now. He never promised her ass shit. She just willingly gave up the pussy the first night he hit her up. Then she went along with the no strings, no feelings shit he laid on her.

She even told me about the shit, acting like she didn't want more from Saint. But she wasn't fooling me. She was sick behind not being his bitch. He was the type of nigga that you wanted to claim you whether he was a thug or not.

She couldn't deny the pull that a real ass gangsta like him had.

"I'll be back tomorrow. I'm calling because you know I been in New Orleans, and word is YOUR man's gonna be in town tonight. Thought I'd look out for you." I said, acting like I had her best interests at heart. When I really didn't give a fuck how the hoe felt, sister or not.

"You know his moves like that?" She asked sounding skeptical.

"Nah, I just work at one of his spots." I added. Shit I was only half lying now.

"And he's not MY man so miss me with that." She finally responded back, after a pause like she was thinking about seeing his ass already.

Yeah I been there, done that so I understood why she was stuck on his ass now.

"Well anyway, I'll see you tomorrow." I finished.

"Wait, I forgot... Your *auntie* been trying to get ahold of you." She said and I heard the way she said Auntie.

My sister couldn't stand my aunt. The two weren't related since me and her had different fathers.

Me and my aunt always were close as hell. She felt more like a real sister to me than my actual one did. We were built the same. We looked at shit in life the same way.

Both of us were gonna get the fuck we could out of everyone and everything while we could. Fuck feelings and fuck who didn't like the shit.

I ended the call with my sister and went ahead and dialed my aunt's number next. She was always hype as hell when I came back in town.

My aunt was the only person I ever confided in and told about the niggas I tricked off of. She never judged me or betrayed me. She also had her own shit going on.

I didn't even head back to my hotel room here in New Orleans. The shit I had here didn't compare to the clothes and my belongings I kept at my sisters spot in Houston. I never stayed in a permanent house or let niggas know where I laid my head for too long.

I usually met them out and shit. I fucked up one time when I was younger. I remembered that shit like it was yesterday.

I walked in from being out on a date and a nigga I fucked over was waiting for me in my pitch black apartment. I swear my life flashed before my eyes that night as the nigga held a gun to my head. He made me suck his dick and let him fuck for the last time.

It was all I could do to convince him to not kill my ass. After playing the nigga for a few months and becoming his "ride or die" bitch I ended up skipping out on his ass middle of the night and taking all his shit. I didn't leave any money or dope behind.

It took him a week, but he finally retaliated and that shit stuck with me for good. I might be a lot of things, but I wasn't a dumb bitch.

Once thing I learned from that shit, was a nigga would go crazy behind his money. More than anything else, any bitch, the paper was some shit that a man didn't let go of willingly or forgive about easily.

So I never let that shit happen again. I learned my lesson. I might give out a hotel room, but I switched up hotels and rooms every week. This shit wasn't a hobby it was my way of life.

I ended up having a long ass conversation with my auntie on the ride back home. By the time I ended the call, there was only an hour until I reached Houston.

I planned to pop up on my sister and Saint. That way I could get proof of his cheating.

That stupid bitch NyAsia, was gonna be done with his ass. I already knew her type. The loyal type. The type that didn't put up with a nigga's disloyalty either.

She would be on to the next nigga and Saint would move onto the next bitch in no time. That stupid bitch should know better than try and hold a nigga like him down. After all, he was a real boss.

Someone like him never just settled for the same pussy night after night. That shit was a fairytale.

Saint

I wasn't tripping by the fact Nya ended up coolin at home for the night. I went ahead and headed out to Houston so I could handle some more shit that had come up in the meantime.

So far all the shit had been running smooth and my new team of niggas was putting in some real mothafuckin' work. I was only able to look over the numbers a few times over the past month, but now that I was moving out there for the next few months that shit was gonna change.

I wanted to see how solid these niggas really were before I put any more of my time and energy behind the shit. We needed to be solid as fuck.

I needed both crews from New Orleans and Houston to be ready when the time came to take over new territory. But first they needed to be able to hold shit down with the area we had.

I planned to sit back for a while and keep shit solely between the two states. I was content with that shit for now. This was in my blood now and I never saw myself getting out of the street shit in this lifetime.

So there wasn't a reason for me to hang back and change up now. Just like my daily routine. Even if I moved up out the hood, I would still come through every fucking day. There was real ass shit you couldn't get nowhere else but in the hood. I was a gangsta for life.

First thing in the morning I planned to head over to see the nigga that was in charge out here now. I only picked his ass to handle shit by default because he was the most respected member of the teacm according to my intel.

My man, Drew that I had on the inside before shit went down put me up on this nigga. I would have said fuck it and put his ass in charge instead, but I was trying to really run shit.

My new team needed to buy into the operation first. That way I would have less problems because mothafuckas would focus on eating instead of other bullshit.

I had to give it to Drew, he was the truth. He was a straight beast and made shit happen even though he was the only white boy involved in the operation out here.

That color shit didn't mean a fucking thing to me. The only color I gave a fuck about was green.

Real was real, and a lot of others in his position would have been quick to jump up and try to gain more power. But he was about the fucking team and not himself. That was some loyal shit, you couldn't teach.

I was posted up in the hotel, just unpacking some fresh shit to throw on when one of my phones buzzed. I had all three of my phones laid out near my suitcase. I reached over and picked up the one I used for Houston business.

When I heard a bitch's voice on the other end I was at a loss for words. I didn't remember giving any hoe my number. I usually didn't fuck with a bitch enough to give them a number I was using.

My numbers changed every three months when I got new phones. All my shit was prepaid with cash. Fuck the Feds, I was trying to stay one step ahead. To some it may seem paranoid, and that was good. I needed to stay paranoid as hell to keep my ass outa the pen.

I didn't say shit back to the bitch. When she finally said "Hello" the third time added to her name I remembered who the fuck it was.

Hearing it was Toya's ass calling made me chill out a little bit. This hoe wasn't like most the bitches I fucked with. Shawty was all professional and shit.

She worked at the bank and didn't even seem like the type of bitch to fuck with a nigga like me. We fucked around a few times when I was in town. She was straight, but nothing compared to my own bitch.

I finally said, "Sup". Shit she called me, she could tell me why she was calling. I already had a pretty good idea.

"Well, I was just thinking of you." She said all timid and shit.

That was the shit I liked to hear. The way Toya spoke was all innocent and shit. That was the reason I fucked with her more than one time. She always did what the fuck I said no questions. She didn't know how to handle my dick at first but shawty could eat the mothafucka.

That was why I went ahead and told her ass to come over to the spot and fuck with ya boy. I hung up with her right after I gave the room number.

I wasn't gonna fuck the bitch but she could give me some brain. I was gonna do right by Nya and that shit meant staying faithful. It was certain shit you didn't do, so I would keep my dick out of any bitch's pussy besides hers.

Shit her pussy was better than all these hoes combined. So it wasn't shit to me.

I finished changing and then poured a drink of Remy. I turned on the big ass TV to sports center and kicked back on the bed relaxing.

I sent Nya a text and then turned off my main phone. I didn't wanna disrespect her by talking all that loving shit and then let a bitch come suck me off. A part of me already knew that to her she would consider a bitch even being in my presence cheating.

Nya didn't take shit from anybody. She was stone cold when it came to her feelings, so I wasn't about to take a chance, even giving her a hint of what I was up to. I knew eventually I would have to get rid of all the bitches and not let none of them even bless me with the brains.

But right now my bitch wasn't here and the way we had been fucking I needed to get this nut off.

I sat back and sipped on the drink in my hand. I could appreciate the hotels and lifestyle I lived. Now that I took the chance and Nya was mine, I really felt like I was on top of the world. The big ass suite I was in had a nice rooftop terrace and shit.

I just hoped that shit lasted and nothing got in the way or fucked up my plans for the future. I was always ready for some shit to pop off, but now that I was at the top of my game all the way around I had more to lose.

I still took all the same precautions so all I could do was hope that it was enough. The hotel room was even booked under a different name using the fake ID I kept for out of town stays and I paid cash for the shit like I usually did. I never traveled under my real government.

Just like I never made any sales on the streets myself when I was hustling on the block. I always had one of the niggas that liked to get a hit do that shit for me. They would make the sale and if their ass got on paperwork, they ended up missing.

Shit worked out most the time. But the case I caught and did time behind still came from that shit. So it wasn't foolproof. If the police would've caught me doing the shit and being hands on with it, it would've tripled my bid.

Now I wanted to stay the fuck outa the penitentiary. My goal was to move even smarter now. I was beyond the street level anymore and didn't have to push weight like that.

Once I got up with my connect that shit was a wrap, but niggas were always questionable about keeping their fucking mouth shut. So only time would tell.

A couple hours later I heard a knock on the door. I had my piece on me and looked through the peephole first. It was just the bitch that I told to come by.

I went ahead and opened the door to let Toya in and then put my tool back under the pillow on the bed when she wasn't looking.

She always tried to act all innocent and I would have let shit play out like I did the few time we hooked up. But now shit was different. I wasn't trying to fuck.

I was ready for her to do what she was gonna do and bounce. I wasn't trying to disrespect my girl.

Toya was light skinned and sexy in a boujie way. She favored Nya a little bit but their personalities were completely different.

I didn't even know this bitch, but knew she wasn't from the hood whatsoever. She was an uppity hoe that came from money. But pussy was pussy and a mouth was all the same to me.

I used to fuck these bitches good and give them that gangsta dick, but only my bitch was gonna get that shit now.

Toya was thick all over and kept her hair short. The shit worked for her. She was beautiful with a flawless body. I backed her up against the foot of the bed to where the back of her knees pressed against it.

Then I put my hands on her shoulders and pressed down. She was already short as fuck compared to me. I was a tall ass nigga over six foot and she only came up to my chest.

She sat her ass down and I dropped my fucking pants. I held her neck from the back and let the bitch do the rest.

When I say this bitch could eat the dick that shit was the mothafuckin' truth. She sucked and worked her mouth. All I could feel was the back of her throat and the suction from her slurping and sucking.

I started moving her head faster and after vibrating her throat on my shit I pulled out and jacked my dick on the hoe's face.

She kissed the tip of my dick and stood up walking to the table beside the bed where there was tissue. She was turned around and started getting undressed.

Yeah the hoe came to get the business, She had on a white thong and matching bra. She bent over and touched her toes making her ass bounce and clap with her shit still on.

I ran my hand over my fade and then pulled my pants back up. It was time for shawty to go. I wasn't gonna fuck no matter how bad lil baby was or how right she got me.

"Yo, I got some shit to handle. I'll get up with you later." I lied my ass off.

I didn't give a fuck about this bitch's feelings but I wasn't trying to sit here and comfort her either. I knew an emotional hoe when I met one.

Toya was straight, but she was weak as fuck. She wasn't built for a nigga like me. I could tell the bitch never even been around thugs her whole life until she fucked with me.

I almost shook my head thinking about how clueless she was to this shit. But I wasn't that nigga, I wasn't her nigga to be giving a fuck one way or the other about how naïve the bitch was.

I didn't show these hoes feelings, because I didn't feel shit for them. I always told them from the jump what it was, so the shit was on them not me.

"Oooookay..." She said with a little attitude that I wasn't even trying to check.

I didn't go back in forth with nobody whether a nigga or a bitch. If I said some shit, I meant that shit end of story. She didn't need to know that the business I needed to handle was taking a shower and going to fucking sleep.

As fucked up as it was, I wasn't gonna return the favor and eat the bitch's pussy or give her the dick. I got what I wanted from her. Now it was time for her to leave.

I handed her back the shirt she took off that was laying on the bed. She went ahead and got dressed in record time. She was acting salty as hell. This would probably be the last time I saw her ass.

I wasn't gonna call her. Shit I wasn't the one that got up with her ass this time. She was the one that set this shit up and wanted to please a nigga.

Right before she got to the door and was about to turn the handle there were loud ass sounds coming from the hallway. My hand immediately went to my back, but my heat was still under the pillow.

I hurried the fuck back towards the bed and grabbed the shit. Before I could see what the fuck was going on or make a move, there were shots coming my way, spraying through the door.

I tried to get out the way, but I wasn't fast enough. I was hit and the painful ass burning in my stomach caused me to drop to the floor.

My stomach and chest were on fire and when I looked down, blood poured out of where I was hit.

I began fading out of consciousness from the lightheadedness and pain. I was able to hear a high pitched scream in the background and some niggas just outside the door yelling some shit.

They were closer than the other surrounding sounds. The scream sounded familiar as hell and I felt the need to see what the fuck was going on.

I couldn't just lay here and go out like this. I tried to pull myself up, but my vision started fading out faster. My arms buckled, and I fell face first again before there was nothing but darkness.

Nya

I just touched down from the last minute flight I booked.

Saint set up a bank account for me when I first got in town. So far, every week there was a $10,000 deposit made each Friday.

I tried to talk shit about the amount of money and get Saint to relax with the shit. But it was necessary for my first tuition bill that I got after signing up for classes. So I shut my damn mouth as soon as Saint grilled my ass back about it.

He didn't even have to let shit come out his mouth, from the way he looked at me when I mentioned it to him.

At least it was coming in handy now. I arrived in no time since it was a short ass flight. It was almost midnight and I was tired as hell but for my man I was gonna do what it took to pull this shit off. He was about to get the best head and pussy and he didn't even expect a damn thing.

I had a rental car already ready and waiting. I booked that shit right along with my flight. I knew my way around Houston from living here, so I was gonna drive myself.

I drove downtown to the hotel Saint was staying at. I couldn't wait to see his reaction when I surprised his ass. A part of me was on edge about the shit though.

I was a real ass bitch and to be honest with myself I went ahead and admitted that he could be laid up with another bitch right now.

Saint was a fine nigga and the whole way he carried himself let everyone know he was a paid. He was a catch and hoes were always more than willing to come up out of their clothes to spend a night with a nigga like him.

I had seen the shit so many times firsthand with the ballers around town and none of them were anywhere near Saint's status. I needed to prepare myself for seeing him cheating with another bitch, just in case.

That was just how I trained my damn brain, to always be prepared for the worst shit and have a plan in place. That way no shit could surprise me. It was how I went about my life on the daily and got through some of the worst times.

I stepped out the car and grabbed my small duffle bag and purse that I brought with me. I didn't check bags or shit. I was only staying a day. Plus even if I was here longer it took longer to get your bags from luggage and I wanted to get to Saint as soon as possible.

As crazy as it sounded I really did miss his ass, just knowing he was away from me and I wasn't gonna see him tonight had me feeling down and shit. I was anxious to see my nigga. It had only been since this morning that I saw him, but the way this nigga turned my ass out and had me feening for the dick was no joke.

As I walked through the lobby I could have sworn I saw that same hoe that was up in VIP at Saint's birthday, when we were out at the club. But I didn't get a good look at who it was since she was far away on the other side of the room, near the back doors.

Maybe I was just paranoid since I had been preparing myself for him to be here with another woman. As soon as I turned to look again from giving the woman working the counter my ID nobody was there. I just attributed it to my mind playing tricks on me and shrugged the shit off.

I always tried to go with my gut, so I did look behind me every so often while I made my way towards Saint's room. I attempted not to look suspicious to mothafuckas and at the same time make sure I wasn't being followed.

Personally, I had never been set up but I knew plenty of bitches that set up niggas all the time. I wasn't a fool and knew that Saint had to have enemies and be stepping on toes if he was moving out to Houston.

All the niggas I knew out here worked for one man. The same nigga that Jaquan used to work for. Jaquan always acted like he was really about that life. But his ass wasn't built to be the gangsta he was pretending to be. I mean he was straight as a corner boy or some shit, but he was all talk mostly. He was too weak to run shit.

I knew his brother worked for the nigga that ran shit too, but I had never met either of his two brothers even though they stayed city.

I shook off the thoughts of the nigga that was now dead thanks to me and Saint. After walking off of the elevator, I was finally less paranoid since not seeing a sole follow me down the hallways downstairs, or the other corridors.

Saint's room was down at the end of the hall. The entire floor was all his since he booked the penthouse suit. I knew his ass was gonna book the best shit.

Just as I finished knocking on the room door, a nigga came out of nowhere behind me and grabbed ahold of my hands, covering my mouth with his other hand.

Three niggas in ski masks caught my ass by surprise. They didn't even make a fucking sound until it was too late.

While the one man had a hold on me, another moved back to the elevator and the other came over close to where I was being held in front of the door.

I tried to fight the nigga off and kicked and strained against the one who was holding onto me. If I could only get to my razor, I could do some damage. But the fuck nigga had my arms and hands locked in a hold behind my back still.

Then the nigga next to us pulled his gun and opened fire right at the door. Since my head was so close to the one shooting and his big ass weapon, my ears started ringing. Bullets were airing out the hotel room in front of me.

It clicked in my head, that they were shooting at the door, probably trying to hit Saint.

I attempted to scream trying to warn him, hoping it wasn't too late, through the hand covering my mouth. But then next thing I felt was a hit to my leg from a bullet and a punch to the face knocking me unconscious.

I started to regain consciousness after who knows how long, and slowly wake back up. I was outside on the street level of the hotel. There were two arms pulling me along while I was laid out being dragged across the cold cement.

I thought of how they were doing all this shit without any body seeing me or stopping them.

My vision started returning more and more. My leg hurt bad as hell and my head was throbbing,

I realized that we were on the backside of the hotel and it was still dark as hell out, meaning too much time had passed, since it was still night.

Both the niggas I was with pulled me behind a dumpster and then dropped me on the ground.

The brunt pain from the impact didn't phase me. Instead, my thoughts went to Saint and I said a quick silent prayer begging God to let him be okay.

I tried to get my nerve up and forget about the horrible pain I was feeling. I needed to find a way to get the fuck away from these niggas. I tried to reach for the razor that was in my hair earlier since I kept in the messy bun.

Right before I was able to touch my hair and see if it was still in place one of the niggas grabbed my hands and held them in place over my head.

I turned my head and wriggled my body trying to get free from the grasp he had on me. Both of the men still had ski masks on.

The one holding my arms said some shit in my ear while he crouched down lower.

"You shoulda knew I was gonna find your ass." Then I was hit straight in the face with blow after blow raining on me from the nigga's fist.

I struggled to keep consciousness and started screaming. I couldn't go out like this. I needed to make sure Saint was good. I needed to kill these niggas.

As soon as I let off that scream, the nigga that was by my side put his pistol down my throat. I started choking on the shit and couldn't make a sound.

I still continued coming in and out of consciousness. Then realized that the other man was now lifting me up and pressing me against the dumpster's side while bringing up my dress.

I had come ready to surprise my man. I tried to scream again even with the barrel of the gun down my throat.

Then the one holding me hit me in the temple one more time, the last time.

Everything went black again, but this time for good.

One week later...

Unknown

The hit went off almost perfect. This bitch was so damn clueless. She thought she was gonna move on with her life, but I would never let that shit happen.

A week passed since I laid her nigga out. I sat back and watched every fucking thing play out just like I planned.

Now I was onto the next target. I sat back watching and waiting from the rental in the hospital parking lot.

It was only a matter of time until I touched every mothafucka in her life and her damn soul. I wasn't gonna make shit easy on her. I wasn't gonna make it quick either. I wanted to take my time and watch the bitch lose her mind behind this shit.

By the time I finished with NyAsia Miller she would wish she never even breathed her first breath. There wasn't nothing and no fucking body that was gonna be able to stop me from making her pay.

They say you shouldn't play with fire, because you'll get burned. And that's exactly what the fuck I was, FIRE.

I was gonna burn this bitch's whole life to the ground. She was gonna wish for death. Only then would I give her an out and kill the bitch.

To be continued...

Books By EL Griffin

Hood Series

Hood Love and Loyalty 1
Hood Love and Loyalty 2
Hood Love and Loyalty 3

Gangsta Love Series

A Gangsta's Pledge

Made in United States
Orlando, FL
15 July 2022